MISTRESS BY ARRANGEMENT

MISTRESS BY ARRANGEMENT

BY

HELEN BIANCHIN

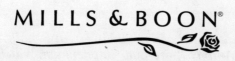

MILLS & BOON®

First published in Great Britain 1999
Large Print edition 2000
Harlequin Mills & Boon Limited,
Eton House, 18-24 Paradise Road,
Richmond, Surrey TW9 1SR

© Helen Bianchin 1999

ISBN 0 263 16367 9

Set in Times Roman 17 on 19 pt.
16-0002-40567

Printed and bound in Great Britain
by Antony Rowe Ltd, Chippenham, Wiltshire

CHAPTER ONE

MICHELLE sipped superb Chardonnay from a crystal wineglass and cast an idle glance at the room's occupants.

The men were resplendent in black dinner suits, white dress shirts and black bow ties, while the women vied with each other in designer gowns.

This evening's occasion was a simple dinner party for ten guests held in the beautiful home of their hosts, Antonia and Emerson Bateson-Burrows, whose reputation for providing fine wine, excellent food, and scintillating company was almost unequalled in Queensland's Gold Coast society.

'Another drink, darling?'

She felt the proprietorial clasp of Jeremy's arm along the back of her waist.

Mine, the action seemed to shriek. The fond glance of his parents, *hers,* merely served to endorse their approval.

Did they think she was unaware of the subtle manipulative matchmaking attempts of late? It was too much of a coincidence that Jeremy had been a fellow guest at several social events she'd attended in the past four weeks.

Marriage wasn't on her agenda, nor was she willing to drift into a meaningless relationship. Thanks to an annuity from her maternal grandmother, her life was good. At twenty-five, she owned her own apartment, ran a successful art gallery in partnership with a friend, and she had no inclination to change the status quo.

She felt the faint pressure of Jeremy's hand at her waist and she summoned a polite smile. 'Thanks, but I'll wait until dinner.'

Which would be when? Were all the guests not accounted for? Speculation rose as she glimpsed Jeremy's mother spare her wrist-watch a surreptitious glance.

Who would dare to be late for a Bateson-Burrows soiree?

'Mother is becoming a tad anxious,' Jeremy revealed, sotto voce. 'Nikos warned he might be unavoidably late.'

Curiosity sparked Michelle's interest. 'Nikos?'

Jeremy cast her an amused look. 'Alessandros. Greek origin, relatively new money, respectably earned,' he added. 'Electronics. Bases in Athens, Rome, Paris, London, Vancouver, Sydney.'

'If his Australian base is in Sydney, what's he doing on the Gold Coast?'

'He has a penthouse in Main Beach,' Jeremy enlightened. 'The man is a consummate strategist. Word has it he's about to close an enviable deal.' His mouth formed a cynical twist. 'Instead of flying directly to Sydney, he's chosen to negotiate from the Gold Coast.'

'Impressive,' she acknowledged, summoning a mental image of a short, paunchy, balding middle-aged Greek with a stylish much younger wife.

'Very,' Jeremy declared succinctly. 'Father covets his patronage and his business account.'

'And his friendship?'

'It's at an adequate level.'

Adequate presumably wasn't good enough, and Emerson Bateson-Burrows' extended invitation to dine was merely part of a larger plan.

Politics, business and social, involved an intricate strategy of a kind that occasionally sickened her altruistic mind.

'Two hours to dine and socialise over coffee,' Jeremy inclined. 'Then we can escape and go on to a nightclub.'

It irked her that he took her acquiescence for granted. She was on the point of telling him so, when some sixth sense alerted her attention.

Curious, she lifted her head and felt the breath catch in her throat.

'Nikos,' Jeremy informed her, although she barely registered the verbal identification as her interest was captured by the tall male figure who had just entered the room.

He possessed broad-boned features, a strong jaw, and his mouth was chiselled perfection.

A man, Michelle perceived with instinctive insight, who wore the fine clothes of a gentleman, possessed the requisite good manners...and had the heart of a predatory warrior.

It was evident in his stance, the cool assessing quality in those dark slate-grey eyes as they roamed the room and its occupants.

They flicked towards her, paused, then settled in a slow appraisal of her dark honey-blond hair, green eyes, and the slender feminine curves encased in a black designer dress.

There was no power on earth that could suppress the faint shivery sensation feathering its way down her spine at the intensity of that look. She felt as if it stripped away the conventional barrier of clothes, lingerie, and stroked her skin.

It took considerable effort to match his appraisal, but she was damned if she'd concede him any sort of victory by glancing away.

Dark hair, well-groomed. Broad shoulders beneath expensive tailoring, and his shoes were hand-tooled leather. In his mid-thirties, he was the antithesis of the middle-aged paunchy balding man Michelle had envisaged.

She watched as he worked the room during an introductory circuit, noting the undoubted charm, the easy smile, an easy grace of movement that implied a high level of physical fitness.

'Michelle Gerard,' Antonia announced by way of introduction, reaching their side. 'Jeremy's girlfriend.'

Nikos Alessandros reached forward, took hold of her hand, and raised it to his lips.

Michelle's eyes flew wide with shock as he placed a brief open-mouthed kiss to her palm, then he curled her fingers as if to seal in the flagrant action. Heat flooded her veins, coursing through her body as each nerve-end sprang into vibrant life.

'Michelle.' His voice held a faint inflection, an accent that was more international than indicative of his own nationality.

Primitive alchemy, potent and incredibly lethal, was a compelling force, and her skin burned where his lips had touched.

'We meet again.'

Again? She'd never met him in this lifetime. If she had, she'd remember. No woman alive could possibly forget someone of Nikos Alessandros' calibre!

Michelle was at once conscious of Antonia's surprised gaze coupled with Jeremy's sharp attention.

'You've already met?'

'While Michelle was studying at the Sorbonne in Paris,' Nikos declared with knowledgeable ease.

A calculated guess? Somehow she doubted it. Which immediately drew the question as to how he came by the information.

'Really?' Antonia queried lightly after a few seconds silence.

Michelle watched in fascination as he directed her a blatantly sensual smile. 'How could I forget?'

She should refute they'd ever set eyes on each other, and accuse him of being a sexist opportunist.

'Your capacity to remember surprises me.' That much was true, yet as soon as the words left her lips she wondered at the wisdom of playing his game.

Midsummer madness? An attempt to alleviate the matchmaking techniques employed by two sets of parents? Or just plain devilry.

Nikos' eyes never left her own, and she experienced the uncanny sensation he could read her mind. Worse, that he could dissect the conventional barriers she'd learnt to erect and divine the path to her soul.

It wasn't a comfortable feeling. But then, she doubted there was anything *comfortable* about this man.

Dangerous, occasionally merciless, powerful. And rarely predictable. A tiny imp added, incredibly sexual. An earthy, uninhibited lover who would seek every liberty, and encourage a similar response. Demand, she amended with instinctive knowledge.

Just the thought of what he could do to a woman, and how he would do it was enough to raise all her fine body hairs in a gesture of...what? Self-preservation? *Anticipation?*

Her eyes dilated at a highly erotic image, one that was so evocative she was unable to subdue the flare of heat from her innermost core.

'Indeed?' That deep drawl held a wealth of meaning she didn't even want to explore.

Antonia sensed it, and immediately launched into an attempt at damage control. 'Nikos, you must allow Emerson to get you a drink.' She placed a hand on his sleeve, and for a moment Michelle held her breath at the possibility he might detach Antonia's hand and opt to stay where he was.

Something moved in his expression, then he smiled, inclining his head in mocking acquiescence as he allowed his hostess to steer him away.

The electric force-field evident didn't diminish, and it took considerable effort to lift the glass to her lips and take a sip of wine.

'You know him.'

Michelle's lips parted to deny it, only to pause fractionally too long.

'And to think I've been playing the gentleman,' Jeremy drawled silkily, raising his glass in a silent mocking salute as he conducted a slow encompassing survey from the top of her head to the tip of her toes and back again.

Indignation heightened the dark golden sparks in her green eyes, and anyone who knew her well would have heeded the silent warning.

'One has only to look at Nikos to know his *friendship* with women is inevitably of an intimate nature.'

'Really?' Michelle tempered the query with a deceptive smile. She wanted to hit him. 'You'd dare to accuse me on the strength of another man's reputation?'

Antonia Bateson-Burrows' announcement that dinner was ready proved opportune.

'Can you blame me for being jealous?' Jeremy offered as they crossed to the dining room.

Nikos Alessandros had a lot to answer for, she determined wryly.

Unbidden, her gaze shifted to the tall male Greek a few feet distant, and she watched in fascinated surprise as he turned briefly towards her.

Those dark slate-grey eyes held an expression she couldn't fathom, and for one infinitesimal second everything faded to the periphery of her vision. There was only *him*. The subdued chatter, the other guests, were no longer apparent.

A slight smile curved his lips, but his eyes remained steady, almost as if he withheld a knowledge of something she couldn't even begin to presume.

The breath caught in her throat, and she deliberately broke the silent spell by transferring her attention to the proposed seating arrangements.

With any luck, Nikos Alessandros would be at the opposite end of the table, precluding the necessity to indulge in polite conversation.

An accomplished hostess, Antonia skilfully manoeuvred her guests into chairs, shuffling them so there were six on one side with five on the other, while she and Emerson took their position at the head of the table.

Oh *hell*. Thirteen at the dinner table on Friday the thirteenth. Could it get any worse?

Don't tempt Fate by even *thinking* about it, a tiny voice taunted, only to discover she faced Nikos across a decorative floral centrepiece.

Emerson poured the wine while Antonia organised the serving of the first course.

'*Salute.*' Nikos' accent was flawless as he lifted his glass, and although his smile encompassed everyone seated at the table, his eyes remained fixed on Michelle.

The soup was delicious vichyssoise, although after the first spoonful Michelle's tastebuds seemed to go on strike.

Succulent prawns in a piquant sauce were served on a bed of mesclan lettuce, and she sipped the excellent white wine, then opted for chilled water in the need for a clear head.

The conversation encompassed a broad spectrum as it touched briefly on the state of the country's financial budget, the possibility of tax reform and its effect on the economy.

'What is your view, Michelle?'

The sound of that faintly accented drawl stirred her senses. Her hand paused midway in its passage from the table to her lips, and her fingers tightened fractionally on the goblet's slim stem.

'Inconsequential, I imagine. Given that whatever my opinion, it will have little effect in the scheme of things.'

Jeremy's silent offer to refill Nikos' glass was met with an equally silent refusal.

The fact that Nikos declined didn't halt Jeremy's inclination to fill his own glass.

'Nevertheless, I would be interested to hear it.'

Having set the cat among the pigeons, it's a source of amusement for you to watch the outcome, she surmised silently. But what if one of the pigeons was unafraid of the cat? Two could play this game.

'As I recall, you were never particularly interested in my mind.'

His eyes held hers, mesmeric in their intensity. She watched as his lips parted to reveal even white teeth, and noticed the movement deepened the vertical slash on each cheek.

'Could anyone blame me, *pedhi mou?*'

His drawled endearment curled round her nerve-ends and sent them spiralling out of control.

'I'll serve the main course.'

Michelle heard Antonia's words, and watched absently as the hired help cleared plates and cutlery and replaced them.

'Some more wine, Nikos?'

Emerson, ever the genial host, merely warranted the briefest glance. 'Thank you, no.' He returned his attention to Michelle. 'I haven't the need for further stimulation.'

This was getting out of hand. It was also gaining the interest of everyone seated at the table.

Chicken in a lemon sauce accompanied by a selection of braised vegetables did little to tempt Michelle's flagging appetite, and she sampled a few mouthfuls of chicken, took a delicate bite of each vegetable, then set down her cutlery.

Water, not wine, was something she sipped at infrequent intervals as she wished fervently for the evening to end.

Yet there was dessert and the cheeseboard to complete the meal, followed by coffee. It would be at least another hour before she could make some excuse to leave.

Jeremy leaned towards her and placed an arm along the back of her chair.

'Tell me, darling.' His voice was a conspiratorial murmur. 'Is he incredibly physical in bed?'

She didn't deign to answer, and deliberately avoided glancing in Nikos' direction as she conversed with the guest seated next to her. Afterwards she had little recollection of the topic or her contribution.

Dessert was an exotic creation of baklava, together with fresh fruit and brandied cream.

Michelle passed on both, and selected a few grapes to freshen her palate.

'Shall we adjourn to the lounge for coffee?' Antonia queried when it appeared everyone had had their fill.

They were the sweetest words Michelle had heard in hours, and she subdued her enthusiasm as she stood to her feet and joined her parents.

Chantelle Gerard cast her daughter a thoughtful glance. 'I had no idea you knew Nikos Alessandros.'

Money was important. Breeding, equally so. The Bateson-Burrows possessed both. But the Alessandros' fortune couldn't be ignored.

Michelle could almost see the wheels turning in her mother's brain. 'I intend leaving very soon.'

'You're going on somewhere with Jeremy, darling?'

'No.'

'I see,' Chantelle voiced sagely. 'We'll talk in the morning.'

'Believe me, *Maman,* there is absolutely nothing to tell,' Michelle assured with an edge of mockery, watching as her mother lifted one eyebrow in silent chastisement. 'Nothing,' she added quietly.

Twenty questions at dawn wasn't her favoured way to begin the day. However, Chantelle was well-practised in the art of subtle manipulation, and Michelle was able to interpret every nuance in her mother's voice.

'We can easily give you a lift home if you're prepared to wait awhile.'

She should have brought her own car. Except Jeremy had insisted he collect her. Not a wise move, she decided wryly in retrospect.

The mild headache she'd thought to invent was no longer a figment of her imagination. And Jeremy was fast becoming a nuisance. Her apartment was less than a kilometre away, a distance she'd entertain no qualms in walking during the day. However, the night hours provided a totally different context for a woman alone.

'I'll call a taxi.'

Antonia offered a superb blend of coffee, together with liqueur, cream, milk, exotic bite-sized continental biscuits and a variety of Belgian chocolates.

Michelle added milk and sugar, and sipped it as quickly as etiquette allowed. Placing her cup and saucer down onto a nearby side-table, she turned towards her hosts, and her stomach executed a slow somersault as she discovered Antonia and Emerson deep in conversation with Nikos Alessandros.

Just pin a smile on your face, thank them for a pleasant evening, and then exit the room. Two or three minutes, five at the most.

Almost as if he sensed her hesitation, Nikos lifted his head and watched her approach.

Jeremy appeared at her side and draped an arm over her shoulder. His hand lingered a hair's-breadth from her breast, and she stepped sideways in an effort to avoid the familiarity, only to have Jeremy's hand close firmly over her arm.

'Finished doing the duty thing with your parents?'

She took exception to his tone, and his manner. 'I don't regard talking to my parents as a duty.'

'You obviously don't suffer parental suffocation as a result of being the only child,' he alluded cynically.

'No,' she responded evenly.

'Ready to leave?' Nikos queried smoothly as she joined Jeremy's parents. 'If you'll excuse us,' Nikos announced imperturbably to his hosts. 'Michelle and I have some catching up to do.' He caught hold of her hand and drew her forward, inclined his head towards a startled Jeremy, then led her from the lounge.

'What do you think you're doing?' she hissed as soon as they reached the foyer.

'Providing you with a lift to your apartment.'

'Michelle.' Jeremy drew level with them. '*I'll* take you home.'

She felt like hitting each of them. One for being overly possessive and childishly jealous. The Greek for his arrogance.

'There's no need to leave your parents' guests,' Nikos intoned pleasantly. 'Michelle's apartment building is almost opposite my own.'

How did he know that?

'She's *my* girlfriend,' Jeremy reiterated fiercely as he turned towards her.

This was getting worse by the second.

'Michelle?' Nikos' voice was silk-encased steel.

Jeremy's hand closed over her shoulder, as if staking a claim. 'Damn you, *tell him.*'

'There's nothing to tell,' she assured quietly, and winced as Jeremy's hold tightened.

'I don't think so, my friend,' Nikos drawled with dangerous softness, and Jeremy

turned towards him with emboldened bellig-
erence.

'This is none of your business!'

'I disagree.'

'Why would you do that?'

'Because Michelle is with me.'

'Damned if she is!' Jeremy's face contorted with fury.

'You want proof?' Nikos demanded silkily.

Michelle didn't get the chance to say a
word in protest as Nikos drew her into his
arms and covered her mouth with his own.

Possessive and frankly sensual, he took advantage of her surprise to taste and plunder
at will, then before she could protest he gathered her close and turned the kiss into something incredibly erotic.

Her heart jumped, then raced to a quick-
ened beat as one hand slid to hold fast her
nape while the other cupped her bottom and
brought her into startling contact with hard
male arousal.

Each and every one of her senses intensified as he sought her response.

Passion...electric, magnetic, *shameless,* it tore through all the conventional barriers to a primitive base that was wholly sexual.

It was as if an instinctive knowledge existed between them, she registered dimly. Something that sanctioned the way his mouth wreaked havoc with her own.

She was supremely aware of him, everything about him. The faint layers of texture and smell heightened her senses...the subtle tang of his cologne, the texture of his skin, the fine fabric of his clothing.

There was a part of her that wanted to travel with him wherever this sensual path might lead, while the sensible *sane* part registered alarm.

With a groan of disgust she dragged her mouth away. Her breathing was ragged, and for the space of a few seconds she had no knowledge of where she was. There was only the man, and a mesmeric helpless hunger.

'What in hell do you think you're doing?'

Jeremy's voice seemed to come from a distance, and she struggled to focus on the immediate present.

'Right now, taking Michelle home,' Nikos declared with deceptive mildness. Without missing a beat he lifted one eyebrow in silent query. 'Michelle?'

Dammit, his breathing was even, steady, while hers seemed as wild and ragged as her heartbeat.

'Walk away from me,' Jeremy warned. 'And I won't have you back.'

She registered Jeremy's rage and felt vaguely sickened. 'You never *had* me in the first place.'

The sound of voices and the appearance in the foyer of two other guests had a diffusing effect, and Jeremy's expression underwent an abrupt change from anger to affability.

'Let's get the hell out of here,' Nikos instructed quietly, taking hold of her arm.

He led her down the few steps to the drive-way, and she made a futile effort to wrench her arm free from his grasp as they drew abreast of a large BMW.

'Don't,' he warned silkily. 'You'll only hurt yourself.'

It was difficult to determine his expression in the dim half-light as he withdrew a set of keys, unlocked the door, then handed them to her. 'Drive, if it will make you feel safer to be with me.'

The soft crunch of gravel as footsteps approached intruded, and she stood stiffly as they drew close.

'Goodnight, Michelle. Nikos.'

Nikos returned the acknowledgement as the couple slid into the car immediately behind them, and in an unbidden gesture Michelle thrust the keys at him, then she un-latched the door and slid into the passenger seat.

Nikos took his position behind the wheel, fired the engine, then eased the car onto the road. Minutes later the powerful car entered the main northbound highway, traversed it for less than a kilometre, and took the next turnoff that led into suburban Main Beach.

She was supremely conscious of him, the slight flash of gold on his wrist as he handled the wheel.

'We'll stop at a café for coffee,' Nikos informed as they paused at a set of traffic lights. 'There's something I'd like to discuss with you.'

'The subtle ''your apartment or mine?'' spiel?' Michelle mocked with light sarcasm. 'Forget it. One-night stands aren't my thing.'

'I'm relieved to hear it.'

The lights changed, and within minutes the powerful engine purred down a notch as he decelerated and touched the brakes, then he eased the vehicle to a halt.

Michelle reached for the door-clasp, a word of thanks ready to emerge from her lips.

Then she froze.

The underground car park was similar to a multitude of beneath street-level concrete caverns. Except it wasn't *her* apartment car park.

CHAPTER TWO

'WHERE the hell are we?'

'My apartment building,' Nikos drawled. 'It happens to be in a block a short distance from your own.' He opened his door and slid out from behind the wheel.

Michelle copied his actions, and stood glaring at him across the roof of the BMW, then she turned and walked to the sweeping upgrade leading to the main entrance.

'The security gate is activated by a personally coded remote.' He paused a beat, then added with killing softness, 'Likewise, the lift is security coded.'

She swung back to face him, anger etched on every line of her body. 'Kidnapping is a criminal offense. If you don't want me to lay charges, I suggest you allow me free passage out of here. Now,' she added with deadly intent. If she'd been standing close enough, she'd have lashed out and hit him.

Nikos regarded her steadily, assessing her slim frame, the darkness of her eyes. There was no fear apparent, and the thought momentarily intrigued him. Self-defence skills? His own had been acquired and honed to a lethal degree.

'All I want is fifteen, maybe twenty minutes of your time.'

Her heartbeat thudded painfully against her ribs. The car park was well-lit, there were a number of cars lining marked bays, but it was eerily quiet. There was no one to whom she could appeal for help.

Michelle extracted her mobile phone and prepared to punch in the requisite digit that would connect her with Emergency Services and alert the police.

'You have nothing to fear from me.'

His voice was even, and controlled. Too controlled. He emanated an indefinable leashed quality, a watchfulness that only a fool would disregard. And she didn't consider herself a fool.

'I don't find this—' she swept an arm in silent indication of her surroundings '—in the least amusing.'

'You were averse to joining me in more comfortable surroundings,' he posed silkily.

Anger meshed with indignation, colouring her features and lending her eyes a fiery sparkle. 'Forgive me.' Her voice dripped icy sarcasm. 'For declining your invitation.'

Her passion intrigued him. Dammit, *she* intrigued him. Most women of his acquaintance, aware of his social and financial status, would have willingly followed wherever he chose to lead.

Yet for all that Michelle Gerard felt like an angel in his arms and responded with uninhibited fervour, instinct relayed that it wasn't part of an act.

'By your own admission,' Michelle vented with restrained anger. 'You brought me here to talk.'

She needed to shift the balance of control. *Fear* wasn't an option. Although the word in itself was a misnomer. Nikos Alessandros didn't mean her any harm, at least not in the physical sense. Yet when it came to her emotions... Now that was an entirely different ball game, something which irked her unbearably, for how could she be emotionally spellbound by a man who, in a short few hours, had broken every conventional social nicety?

'I suggest you do so, *now,*' she continued forcefully. 'And condense whatever you have to say into two minutes.' She indicated the mobile phone. 'One wrong move and I'll summon the police.'

He leaned one hip against the smooth bonnet of his car, and regarded her thoughtfully.

'I want you to be my social companion for a few weeks,' he stated without preamble.

Michelle drew in a deep breath and released it slowly. Whatever she'd expected, it hadn't been this. He had only to beckon and women would beat a path to his side. 'Surely you jest?'

His attention didn't falter. 'I'm quite serious.'

'Why?'

'For much the same reason it would suit you.'

She didn't pretend to misunderstand. 'What makes you so sure?'

'Body language,' Nikos drawled.

Her eyes flashed golden fire. 'I can handle Jeremy.'

'I don't doubt you can.' One eyebrow lifted. 'The question is, do you want to?'

'I don't need anyone to fight my battles,' she said dryly. 'Any more than you do. So why don't you cut to the chase?'

'I thought I already had.'

Her head tilted to one side. 'You expect me to believe there's a female you can't handle?' The prospect was almost laughable.

'The widow of a very close friend of mine,' Nikos enlightened her slowly. 'Her husband was killed several months ago in a skiing accident.'

'She is emotionally fragile, and genuinely misinterprets the friendship?' Michelle posed. 'Or has she become a calculating vixen intent on snaring another rich husband?'

His expression imperceptibly hardened, a subtle shifting of muscle over bone that reassembled his features into a compelling mask.

'You presume too much.'

So she'd struck a tender nerve. Interesting that he didn't answer her question.

'You feel honour-bound to spare—' She paused deliberately.

'Saska.'

'Saska,' she continued. 'Any embarrassment during what is a transitional grieving period?'

'Yes,' he declared succinctly.

'I see.' She regarded him thoughtfully. 'And on the basis of one meeting, an appraisal of *body language,* you virtually kidnap me and suggest I have nothing better to do with my time than act out a part for your benefit.'

'There would be a few advantages.'

Topaz flecks shone in the depths of her green eyes, a silent evidence of her anger. 'Name one.'

'All of the pleasure and none of the strings.'

'And a bonus, I imagine, if I'm sufficiently convincing?' The flippant query slipped from her lips, and she glimpsed the faint edge of humour tilt the corner of his mouth.

'I'm sure we can come to an amicable arrangement.'

The entire evening had been a complete farce, including Jeremy's behaviour. As for Nikos Alessandros... *Impossible* didn't come close!

'Just who the hell do you think you are?' she demanded fiercely.

His expression hardened slightly, and his eyes took on the quality of steel. 'A man who recognises an opportunity, and isn't afraid to seize it.'

She could still feel the touch of his mouth on hers, his taste…and the way her senses had flipped into a tailspin.

His indolent stance was deceptive. She had the instinctive feeling that if she turned away from him, he would simply reach out and haul her back.

'Go find some other female,' Michelle directed. 'I'm not willing to participate.'

She caught the dark glitter in his eyes, glimpsed a muscle tense at the edge of his jaw, and experienced momentary satisfaction at besting him.

'There's nothing I can do to change your mind?'

Her gaze didn't waver. 'No, not a thing.'

He examined her features with contemplative scrutiny. 'In that case, we'll take the lift to the ground floor and I'll escort you to your apartment.'

She wanted to argue with him, and almost did.

'Wise,' Nikos drawled.

Michelle felt her stomach twist as they stepped into the small electronic cubicle. She was incredibly aware of the emotional pull, the intangible meshing of the senses.

Seconds later she preceded him into the main lobby, passed reception, then emerged into the fresh evening air.

Less than a hundred metres distant lay several trendy restaurants and cafés, each with outdoor chairs and tables lending the area a cosmopolitan air.

Michelle's apartment building was situated fifty metres distant on the opposite side of the road, and when they reached its entrance she paused, a polite smile widening her lips as she turned towards him.

There was nothing to thank him for, and she didn't make a pretense of doing so. The polite smile was merely a concession.

'You forgot something.'

She caught the purposeful gleam in those dark eyes an instant before hands captured her face.

His head descended and his mouth covered hers in a kiss that plundered deep, savouring the inner sweetness without mercy, his tongue swift and incredibly clever as he took his fill.

This was skilled mastery, she registered dimly, and a silent gasp of outrage remained locked in her throat as he cupped her bottom and brought her close up against him so that she was in no doubt of his arousal.

Potent, shimmering heat sang through her veins and pooled at the centre of her feminine core. She could feel the thrust of her breasts as they swelled in anticipation of his touch, their tender peaks hardening into sensitive buds craving the tantalising succour of his mouth.

This was insane. A divine madness that had no place, no basis in *anything*.

Almost as if he sensed her withdrawal, he gradually lightened the kiss to a gentle brush of his lips against her own. Then he lifted his head, and released her.

'Pleasant dreams, *pedhi mou,*' he bade gently.

His eyes were warm, and deep enough to drown in. The flip response she sought never found voice, and she turned away from him, activated the security code on the external door, then hurried into the lobby without a backward glance.

Damn him. He was the most arrogant infuriating devastating man she'd ever met. Infinitely dangerous, she added as she jabbed the call button to summon one of two lifts.

As soon as the doors slid open she entered the cubicle, stabbed the appropriate panel button, and barely suppressed a shiver as the lift sped swiftly upward.

If she never saw him again, it would be too soon. Which was a total contradiction in terms, she grimaced as the lift came to a halt at her floor.

Seconds later she let herself into her apartment, hit the light switch, checked the locking mechanism was in place, then she moved through to the kitchen.

Caffeine would keep her awake, so she opted for a glass of chilled water, sipped the contents, then crossed to her bedroom.

It was several minutes this side of midnight, and she divested her clothes, took a leisurely warm shower, then slid between cool percale sheets in an effort to cull sleep.

Without success. There were too many images crowding her mind. A tall dark-haired Greek whose eyes seemed to haunt her. His voice, with its slightly accented timbre that curled like silk round every sensitive nerve-end, invading without license as a vivid reminder of his touch. The feel of his hands on her body, their caressing warmth, and the taste of his mouth on hers as it devoured, savoured, and sought to imprint his brand.

It was almost as if she could still sense the exclusive tones of his cologne, the clean smell of fine tailoring and fresh laundered cotton. And a subtle masculine scent that was *his...*

Dammit. She didn't want to be this *disturbed* by a man. To have her senses invaded by a pervasive sexual alchemy.

She'd met scores of men, been charmed by several, discovered an affection for a few, and loved none. At least, not the *swept off my feet, melting bones* kind of emotion portrayed on the cinema screen and extolled between the pages of many a romance novel.

When it came to attraction, she was still waiting for the earth to move. Warm and fuzzy somehow didn't come close to hungry shattering sensual sexuality.

Yet tonight she'd experienced it in the arms of a stranger.

For the space of...how long? Two, three minutes? She'd lost all sense of time and place. There was only the man, the moment, and raw unbridled passion.

Her body had curved into his, and clung, moulding in a perfect fit as his mouth had taken possession of her own.

And it had been *possession.* Demanding, compelling, and frankly sensual, his kiss was a promise. Primitive, raw, libidinous.

It should have frightened her. Instead, for the space of those few minutes she'd felt exhilarated, *alive,* and aware. Dear God, so aware of every pulse beat, the heat that flared from every erogenous zone as her whole body coalesced into a throbbing entity, almost totally beyond her control.

If he could initiate such an effect with just a kiss, what sort of lover would he be?

Intensely vital, passionate, and incredibly sensual. Hungry, wild…*shameless,* she added with certainty.

What was she thinking?

Nikos Alessandros was the last man on earth she would want to have anything to do with.

She lifted her head and thumped her pillow. Damn the hateful images invading her mind. They clouded her perspective, dulled commonsense, and played havoc with her nervous system.

All she had to do was fall asleep, and in the morning a fresh new day would dispense with the night's emotional turmoil.

CHAPTER THREE

THE insistent ring of the telephone penetrated Michelle's subconscious, and she reached out a hand, searched blindly for the handset, and succeeded in knocking the receiver onto the floor.

Oh hell. What a way to start the day.

She caught hold of the spiral cord and tugged until her fingers connected with the receiver.

'Michelle.'

Inches away from her ear she recognised the feminine voice, and she stifled an unladylike oath.

'*Maman,*' she acknowledged with resignation. Just what she needed.

'Are you still in bed, *cherie?*' There was a slight pause. 'Do you know what time it is?'

Seven, maybe eight, she hazarded, sparing a quick glance at the bedside clock before drawing a sharp breath. *Nine.*

'You are alone?'

Michelle closed her eyes, then opened them again. 'No, *Maman.* Two lovers have pleasured me all through the night.'

'There is no need to be facetious, darling,' Chantelle reproved, and Michelle sighed.

'I'm sorry. Blame it on lack of sleep.'

'I thought we might do lunch.' Chantelle named a trendy restaurant at Main Beach. 'Shall we say twelve?' And hung up before Michelle had a chance to confirm or refuse.

'Grrr.' The sound was a low-pitched growl that held a mixture of irritation and compliance. She could ring back and decline, except she knew almost word for word what Chantelle would say as a persuasive ploy.

Emotional blackmail of the nicest kind, she added mentally as she replaced the receiver and rolled onto her stomach.

Lunch for her mother inevitably meant a minuscule Caesar salad, followed by fresh fruit, a small glass of white wine and two glasses of water. Afterwards they would browse the trendy boutiques, drive the short distance to Marina Mirage, relax over a leisurely *latte,* then wander at will through the upmarket emporiums.

It was a mother-daughter thing they indulged in together on occasion. Michelle was under no illusion that today's invitation was a thinly-veiled guise to conduct an in-depth discussion about her association with Nikos Alessandros.

In which case she'd best rise, shine and meet the day. Routine chores and the weekly visit to the supermarket would occupy an hour and a half, and she'd need the remaining time to shower and change if she was to meet her mother at noon.

Chantelle ordered her favourite Caesar salad, and mineral water, while Michelle settled for something more substantial.

'Antonia and Emerson have insisted we join them on their boat for lunch tomorrow.'

Sunglasses shielded her mother's eyes, successfully hiding her expression. Although Michelle wasn't fooled in the slightest.

Chantelle had conversation down to a fine art. First there would be the pleasantries, some light humour in the form of an anecdote or two, followed by the main purpose of the meeting.

'That will be nice,' Michelle commented evenly.

'We will, of course, be back in time to attend the Gallery exhibition.'

This month's exhibition featured an up and coming local artist whose work had impressed both Gallery partners. Arrangements for each exhibition were made many months in advance, and it said much for the Gallery's reputation that they had bookings well into next year for future showings.

Emilio possessed an instinctive flair for what would succeed, and their combined talents and expertise had seen a fledging Gallery expand to become one of the most respected establishments on the coastal strip.

Invitations had been sent out to fifty patrons and their partners, the catering instructions had been given. All that remained were the final touches, and placement of the exhibits.

Something which both she and Emilio would attend to this afternoon and complete early tomorrow morning. 'Do you have any plans for tonight, darling?'

Michelle wound a portion of superb fettuccine marinara onto her fork and held it poised halfway above her plate. 'An early night, *Maman*.'

'Oh, I see.'

Did she? 'You know how much effort Emilio and I put into each exhibition,' Michelle said lightly. 'There are so many things to check, and Emilio is particular with every detail.'

'I know, darling.'

Chantelle considered education as something important for Michelle to acquire. The private school, university, time abroad to study at the Sorbonne. Except she really wasn't expected to *do* anything as a result of such qualification and experience.

The Gallery had been viewed as a frivolous venture. Michelle's partnership with Emilio Bonanno was expected to be in name only, something she quickly dispelled as she steadfastly refused to join her mother on the social circuit, confining herself to the occasional charity dinner or gala, much to Chantelle's expressed disappointment.

You could say, Michelle mused, that for the past three years her mother had graciously accepted that her own social proclivities were not shared by her daughter. However, it didn't stop Chantelle from issuing frequent invitations, or, for the past year, indulging in subtle matchmaking attempts.

'I think you've succeeded in making Jeremy jealous.' Chantelle took a sip of mineral water, then set down the glass. 'He wasn't quite himself after you left last night. Has he telephoned you this morning?'

'No,' Michelle responded evenly. 'I don't particularly want to hear from him.'

'Because of Nikos Alessandros?'

'Nikos Alessandros has nothing whatsoever to do with it.'

'He's quite a catch, darling.'

She chose to be deliberately obtuse. 'Jeremy?'

'Nikos,' Chantelle corrected with a tolerant sigh.

'As I have no intention of indulging in a fishing expedition, whether or not he's a catch is totally irrelevant.'

'Do you have time to do a little window shopping?' Chantelle queried. 'I really think I could add something to my wardrobe.'

To give her mother credit, she knew when to withdraw. 'I promised Emilio I'd be at the Gallery at two-thirty.'

Chantelle savoured the last mouthful of cos lettuce, then replaced her fork. 'In that case, darling, do finish your pasta. We'll share a coffee later, shall we?'

Clothes, shoes, lingerie, perfume. Any one, or all four, could prove a guaranteed distraction, and Michelle accompanied her mother into one boutique after another in her quest to purchase.

An hour and a half later Chantelle held no less than three brightly emblazoned carry bags, and there was no time left to share coffee.

'See you tomorrow, darling. Don't work too hard.'

Michelle placed a light kiss on her mother's cheek, then watched as Chantelle stowed her purchases in the boot before crossing to slide in behind the wheel of her Mercedes.

It was almost two-thirty when Michelle entered the Gallery. A converted house comprising three levels, it had been completely renovated. Polished wooden floors gleamed with a deep honey stain, and the walls were individually painted in several different pale colours providing a diverse background for carefully placed exhibits. Skylights threw angled shafts of sunlight, accenting subtle shadows as the sun moved from east to west throughout the day.

She experienced a degree of pride at the decor, and what she'd been able to achieve in the past three years.

'Emilio?'

She returned her keys to her bag and carefully closed the door behind her.

'Up here, *cara,*' an accented voice called from the mezzanine level. 'Brett is with me.'

A short flight of stairs led to the next level. Above that were Emilio's private rooms.

Michelle moved swiftly towards the upstairs studio where Brett's exhibition was to be held. 'Hi,' she greeted warmly as she joined them. Both men glanced up, gave her a penetrating look, then switched their attention to the stack of paintings propped carefully against one wall.

'*Cara,* stand over there, and tell us what you think,' Emilio commanded.

For the next four hours they worked side by side, then when the artist left they ordered in pizza, effected a few minor changes, satisfied themselves that every exhibit was strategically placed according to their original plan.

'He's nervous,' Michelle noted as she bit into a slice of piping hot pizza. Melted cheese, pepperoni, capsicum…delicious.

'It's his first exhibition,' Emilio granted, following her action.

The light glinted in reflection from the ear-stud he wore. Designer stubble was at odds with his peroxided crew cut. A lean sinewy frame clothed in designer jeans and T-shirt, he bore the visual persona of an avant garde. His sexual preferences were the subject for conjecture, and he did nothing to dispel a certain image. However, it was part of the tease, the glamour associated with a role he chose to play, and the knowledge very few close friends knew he was straight and not at all what he appeared to be, only amused him.

Behind the image lay a very shrewd business brain, an almost infallible instinct for genuine talent, and an indefinable *nous* for what appealed to the buying public.

It was something Michelle also shared, and their friendship was platonic, based on mutual knowledge, affection and respect.

'You are pensive. Why?'

Forthright, even confrontational, Emilio possessed the ability to divine whenever anything bothered her. She delayed answering him by pulling the tab on a can of soft drink and taking a long swallow of the ice-cold liquid.

'A man, huh?' Emilio pronounced. 'Do I know him?'

She replaced the can onto the table, and took another bite of pizza. 'What makes you so sure it's a man?'

'You have soft shadows beneath those beautiful green eyes.' His smile was gentle, but far too discerning. 'Lack of sleep, sweetheart. And as you rarely party 'til dawn, I doubt a late night among the social elite was the cause.'

'I could merely be concerned about tomorrow's exhibition.'

'No,' he declared with certainty. 'If you don't want to talk about him, that's fine.'

Michelle cast him a level look. 'He was a guest at a dinner I attended.' She paused fractionally. 'And if I never see him again, it'll be too soon.'

'Trouble,' Emilio accorded softly. 'Definitely.'

'No,' she corrected. 'Because I won't allow him to be.'

'*Cara,* I don't think you'll have a choice.' His quiet laughter brought forth a vexed grimace.

'Why do you say that?'

'Because you're a beautiful young woman whose fierce protection of self lends you to eat lesser men for breakfast,' he mocked. 'The fact you haven't been able to succeed with this particular one is intriguing. I shall look forward to meeting him.'

'It won't happen,' Michelle vowed with certainty.

'You don't think so?'

'I know so,' she responded vehemently.

'OK.' Emilio lifted both hands in a conciliatory gesture, although his smile held humour. 'Eat your pizza.'

'I intend to.' She bit into the crisp crust, then reached forward, caught up a paper napkin and wiped her fingers. 'I'll help you clean up, then I'm going home.'

'An empty pizza carton, a few glasses, soft drink cans. What's to clean?'

'In that case,' she inclined, standing to her feet in one fluid movement. 'I'm out of here.' She leaned forward and brushed her cheek to his. *'Cíao.'*

*   *   *

The Gallery opened at four, and an hour later the full complement of guests had gathered, mingling in small clutches, glass in hand. Taped baroque music flowed softly through strategically placed speakers, a soothing background to the muted buzz of conversation.

Michelle had selected a classic fitted dress in black with a lace overlay. Stiletto heels, sheer black hose, her hair swept high, and understated make-up with emphasis on her eyes completed a picture that portrayed elegance and style.

Hired staff proffered trays containing a selection of hors d'oeuvres, and already a number of Brett's paintings displayed a discreet *sold* sticker.

Success, Michelle reflected with a small sigh of relief. Everything was going splendidly. The finger food couldn't be faulted, the champagne was superb, and the ambience was *perfecto,* as Emilio would say.

She glanced across the room, caught his eye, and smiled.

'Another triumph, darling.'

Her stomach tightened fractionally as she recognised Jeremy's cynical voice, and she summoned a polite smile as she turned to face him. 'I didn't expect you to honour the invitation.'

'I wouldn't have missed it for the world.'

He leaned forward and she moved slightly so that his lips brushed her cheek. An action which resulted in a faint intake of breath, the momentary hardening of his eyes.

'The eminently eligible Nikos has yet to put in an appearance, I see.' He moved back a pace, and ran light fingers down her arm.

Michelle tilted her head a little and met his dark gaze. 'A little difficult, when he wasn't issued an invitation.'

'Dear sweet Michelle,' Jeremy chided with sarcastic gentleness. 'Nikos was an invited guest on the parents' cruiser today. The enchanting Chantelle issued the invitation to your Gallery soiree.' He paused for effect before delivering the punch line. 'As I recall, Nikos indicated he would grace us with his presence.'

Her heart tripped and raced to a quicker beat. 'Really?'

One eyebrow slanted in mockery. 'Am I mistaken, or is that not pleasurable anticipation I sense?' He primed a barb and aimed for the kill. 'Didn't he come up to scratch last night, darling?' His smile held thinly veiled humour. 'Jet lag can have that effect.'

Calm, just keep calm, she bade silently as she moved back a pace. He didn't release her arm, and she gave him a deliberately pointed look. 'This conversation is going nowhere, Jeremy.' She flexed her arm, felt his grip tighten for an instant before he released her. 'If you'll excuse me, I really must mingle.' Her voice assumed an icy formality. 'I hope you enjoy the exhibition. Emilio and I are confident of Brett's talent and potential.'

'Ah, the inimical Emilio,' Jeremy drawled. 'You do know he's bisexual?'

As well as being untrue, it was unkind. She didn't miss a beat. 'Slander isn't a pretty word. Watch you don't find yourself in court on a legal charge.'

'A mite too protective, darling.'

'And you,' she declared with quiet emphasis. 'Are a first-class—'

'Michelle.'

Her body quivered at the sound of that faintly accented voice, and her pulse went into overdrive. How much of her argument with Jeremy had Nikos Alessandros heard?

Everything came into sharp focus as she slowly turned to face him.

'Nikos,' she acknowledged, and imperceptibly stiffened as he placed a hand at the back of her waist.

His expression gave nothing away, but there was a hint of steel beneath the polite facade as he inclined his head.

'Jeremy.'

Michelle's nerves flared into sensitised life at his close proximity.

'Is there a problem?' Nikos asked smoothly, and she felt like screaming.

Yes. Jeremy for behaving badly, and *you* just for being here!

A determined sparkle darkened her eyes. 'If you'll excuse me? I really should mingle.'

She turned away, only to find that Nikos had joined her.

'Just what the hell do you think you're doing?' she queried with quiet vehemence the instant they were out of Jeremy's earshot. She made a concerted effort to shift out of his grasp without success.

'Rescuing you.'

'I didn't need rescuing!'

His smile held a hint of cynical humour. 'Especially not by me.'

'Look—'

'Save the indignation for a more suitable occasion.'

'Why?' Michelle vented with quiet fury. 'When I have no intention of seeing you again.'

'Considering your parents and the Bateson-Burrows have issued me with a few interesting invitations, that's most unlikely,' Nikos assured silkily.

She wanted to hit him. It was enough she had to deal with Jeremy, whose recalcitrance in the past twenty-four hours could be directly attributed to the man at her side.

Had Nikos not been a guest at the Bateson-Burrows' dinner table, she could have conducted a diplomatic discussion last night with Jeremy, and he wouldn't now be behaving quite inappropriately.

Or would he? Jeremy had displayed a side to his personality she'd never suspected might exist.

'Suppose we embark on a conducted tour of your protegé's work.'

'Why?' she demanded baldly, and found herself looking into a pair of amused dark grey eyes.

'I could be a potential buyer, and you do, Chantelle assures me, have an excellent eye for new talent.'

Did she realise just how beautiful she looked when she was angry?

'Mother has excelled herself in lauding my supposed talents,' she stated dryly.

'Cynicism doesn't suit you.'

In any other circumstance, she would have laughed. However, tonight she wasn't in the mood to see the humorous side of Chantelle's machinations.

They drew close to one exhibit, and she went into a professional spiel about light and colour and style, Brett's unusual technique, and indicated the painting's possible worth on the market in another five years.

Nikos dropped his arm from her waist, and she wondered why she suddenly felt cold, even vaguely bereft.

Crazy, she dismissed. Every instinct she possessed warned that Nikos Alessandros was a man she should have nothing to do with if she wanted to retain her emotional sanity.

CHAPTER FOUR

'WHICH of the collection is your personal favourite?' Nikos queried as they moved from one exhibit to another.

There were interruptions as she was greeted by a few guests, and on each occasion good manners demanded she introduce the man at her side.

She could sense their masked speculation, sense their curiosity, and she wasn't sure whether to feel angry or resigned.

Michelle's lips parted to make a flippant response, only to change her mind at the last second. 'The little boy standing on a sandhill looking out over the ocean.'

He lifted a hand and tucked a stray lock of hair back behind her ear. He watched her eyes dilate, and felt the slight shiver his touch evoked. 'Why that particular painting?'

'Because it seems as if the ocean represents his world, and he's curious to know where it ends and what's beyond the horizon. If you look at his features, there's wonderment, excitement.' Her voice softened. 'He's trying not to be afraid, but he is. You can see it in the faint thrust of his lower lip, the way his chin tucks in a little.' She raised her hand, then let it fall again to her side.

It was more than just a painting, it represented life. The promise of what might be. Even though the logical mind relegated the image to the skilled use of paint on canvas and artistic flair.

'Consider it sold.'

Michelle glanced up and examined the chiselled perfection of his features. 'You haven't asked the price.'

'It's listed on the programme.' His smile was wholly sensual. 'What discount are you prepared to offer me?'

She badly wanted to say *none*, except 'business' was a separate category to 'personal,' and anyone with sufficient *nous* en-sured the two were kept apart. 'It depends on your method of payment.'

'I'll present you with a bank cheque at midday tomorrow, and organise delivery.'

Michelle didn't hesitate. 'Five per cent.'

It shouldn't concern her where he intended to hang it, in fact she told herself she didn't care.

'Something is bothering you?'

His light tone didn't fool her in the slightest. He was too intuitive, and she loathed his ability to tune into her thoughts. It made her feel vulnerable, and too acutely sensitive.

'Why should anything bother me? I've just sold the most expensive painting featured in this exhibition.'

'By your own admission, it's the one you admire most,' Nikos pursued softly. 'I imagine you can offer a suggestion how it should be displayed to its best advantage?'

She could tell him to do what he liked with it, but professional etiquette got the better of her.

'It should occupy centre stage on a wide wall,' she opined slowly. 'Preferably painted a very pale shade of blue, so the colours mesh and there's a sense of continuity.'

Interesting, he perceived, that her love of art overcame her instinctive wariness of him.

'Now, if you'll excuse me,' Michelle said purposefully. 'There's something I need to check with my business partner.' She offered him a polite smile, then turned and went in search of Emilio.

'So he's the one,' Emilio said in a quiet aside several minutes later.

'I don't know what you're talking about.'

'Yes, you do.'

'I'd prefer not to discuss it.'

'As you wish.'

'Dammit, I don't even like him!'

'So… What's liking got to do with anything?' Emilio queried mildly.

'Grrr,' she vented softly, and incurred his soft laughter.

'Stephanie.' He was suddenly the businessman, the art entrepreneur, assuming the faintly affected manner he'd honed to perfection. 'How are you, darling?'

Michelle followed suit, according the wealthy widow due deference. The money Stephanie Whitcomb had spent in their Gallery over the past few years went close to six figures.

'Such a success, *cherie,*' Chantelle complimented as Michelle crossed to her parents' side. 'We are very proud of you.'

'Indeed. A stunning exhibition.'

'Thank you, *Papa.* Naturally you're prejudiced.'

Etienne smiled as he leaned forward to bestow a light kiss to her cheek. 'Of course.'

'Tomorrow we're hosting a small cocktail evening. Just very close friends. Six o'clock. You'll join us, won't you?'

Her mother's idea of a small gathering could number anything from twenty to thirty people. Drinks on the terrace, a seemingly casual but carefully prepared finger-food buffet.

'*Maman,* no,' Michelle voiced with regret. 'I have plans.'

'What a shame. We included Saska in Nikos' invitation. I thought you might like to bring Emilio.'

There was a silent message evident which Michelle chose to ignore. 'Another time, perhaps?'

'If you reconsider…' Chantelle trailed delicately.

'Thank you, *Maman.*'

Guests were beginning to drift towards the door, and as always, it took a while for the Gallery to empty.

Michelle organised the hired staff as they packed glassware into containers. Much of the cleaning up had already been done, and Emilio handed over a cheque, then saw them off the premises.

'Go home,' he ordered without preamble. 'You're tired, it shows, and I'll deal with everything in the morning.'

'I had no idea I looked such a wreck,' Michelle said dryly.

'Darling, I am an old friend, and I can tell it like it is,' he said gently.

'It was a successful evening.'

All of Brett's paintings had sold, and they'd succeeded in confirming a tentative date in April to host another exhibition of his work.

'Very,' Emilio agreed, as she reached up and brushed his cheek with her lips. 'For what it's worth, I approve of the Greek.' He lifted a hand and smoothed back a stray tendril of hair that had escaped from the chignon at her nape. 'I enjoyed watching him watch you.'

Something inside Michelle's stomach curled into a tight ball. 'Since when did you become my protector?'

'Since I fell in love with you many years ago…as a sister,' he teased gently.

She smiled with genuine affection. 'In that case, *brother,* I'm going home and leaving you with all that remains of the clean-up chores.'

'Tomorrow morning, ten,' Emilio reminded. 'Take care.'

Her car was parked about twenty metres distant, the street was well-lit, and as the Gallery was situated off the main street housing numerous cafés and restaurants, there were several parked cars in the immediate vicinity.

Michelle gained the pavement and stepped in the direction of her car, only to pause at the sight of a male figure leaning against its bonnet.

The figure straightened and moved towards her. 'I thought you were never going to leave,' Jeremy complained.

She stepped forward to cross the grass verge, and felt his hand grasp her arm.

'It's been a long day, and I'm tired,' she said firmly. Her patience was getting thin, but she recognised a certain quality about him that made her very wary. 'Goodnight.'

'Dammit, Michelle, you can't just walk away from me.'

'Please let go of my arm. I want to get into my car.'

She was unprepared for his sudden movement as he twisted her close with vicious strength, then ground his mouth against her own.

Instinct and training combined to allow her to unbalance him, and one swiftly hooked foot sent him falling to the ground.

Michelle moved quickly round to the driver's side, unlocked the door, and was about to slide into the seat when Jeremy caught hold of her arm and dragged her out.

'I believe the lady said no,' a slightly accented male voice drawled hardily.

Jeremy's fingers tightened with painful intensity, and she could feel his palpable anger.

'Bitch!'

'Let her go,' Nikos commanded with dangerous softness. 'Or else I promise you won't walk easily for days.'

Michelle caught her breath as Jeremy's fingers bit to the bone, then he flung her arm free, turned and crossed the road to his car, fired the engine with an ear-splitting roar, and sent the tyres spinning as he sped down the road.

Nikos said something vicious beneath his breath as she stiffened beneath his touch, and he swore briefly, pithily, in his own language.

Michelle edged the tip of her tongue over her lips and discovered several abrasions where her teeth had split the delicate tissues.

'I'll drive you home.'

'No.' She told herself she didn't need his concern. 'I'm fine.' To prove it, she slid in behind the wheel, only to have him lean into the car and bodily shift her into the passenger seat.

Seconds later he took her place and engaged the ignition.

'There's no need for you to do this,' Michelle asserted as he set the car in motion.

Three blocks and two minutes later he swept through the entrance to her apartment building and paused adjacent the security gate leading to the underground car park.

'Do you have your card?'

She handed it to him wordlessly, and when the gate was fully open she directed him to her allotted space.

'What about your own car?'

He directed her a dark glance as he led her towards the lift. 'I walked.' He jabbed the call button, and when the lift arrived, he accompanied her into it. 'Which floor?'

'There's no—'

'Which floor?' Nikos repeated with dangerous quietness.

He was icily calm. Too calm, she perceived, aware there was something apparent in his stance, the set of his features, that revealed anger held in tight control.

'I appreciate your driving me home. But I'm fine.'

She glimpsed the darkness in his eyes, the hard purpose evident, and was momentarily bereft of speech. 'Really,' she added seconds later.

One eyebrow rose slightly, and she met his silent scrutiny with unblinking equanimity.

'Look in the mirror,' Nikos bade quietly, and watched as she spared the decorative mirrored panel a glance.

Her hair was no longer confined in a neat chignon, her eyes were dark, dilated and seemed far too large in features that were pale, and her mouth was swollen.

'Now, which floor?' he queried with velvet softness, and she hesitated momentarily before capitulating.

'Fifteenth.'

They reached it in seconds, and she silently indicated the door leading to her apartment.

Once inside she had the compelling urge to remove Jeremy's touch from her skin, and she wanted to scrub her teeth, cleanse her mouth.

'I'm going to take a shower and change.' She no longer cared whether Nikos Alessandros was there or not, or whether he'd have gone when she returned. Uppermost was the need to be alone, shed and dispense with her clothes.

Hell, she'd probably burn them, she determined as she reached the bedroom and began peeling each item from her body.

Michelle activated the shower dial and set it as hot as she could bear, then she lathered every inch of skin, rinsed, and repeated the process three times. Satisfied, she turned the dial to cold and let the needle spray revive and revitalise her before she reached for a towel.

Minutes later she donned clean underwear, then reached for jeans and a loose cotton top. She discounted make-up, and applied the hair dryer for as long as it took to remove most of the dampness, then she simply wound it into a knot and pinned it on top of her head.

Michelle walked into the kitchen and saw Nikos in the process of brewing coffee. He'd removed his jacket and his tie. He'd also loosened a few top buttons and folded back the cuffs of his shirt.

His appraisal was swift, yet all-encompassing. 'I've brewed some coffee.'

There were two cups and saucers on the countertop, sugar and milk, and she watched as he filled her cup.

He looked comfortably at ease, yet instinct warned that anger lurked just beneath the surface of his control.

'You don't have to do this.' She hugged her arms together across her midriff, and temporarily ignored the cup and saucer he pushed towards her.

'No,' Nikos responded evenly. 'I don't.' He added sugar to his cup, stirred, then lifted it to his mouth.

She should suggest the more formal surroundings of the lounge, but the last thing she wanted to do was indulge in meaningless conversation.

'Do you intend laying charges?'

Her eyes widened slightly. Oh God, that meant involving the police, filing a complaint. The facts becoming public knowledge. Jeremy's parents, her parents, their friends…

'I don't think so,' she said at last.

His piercing regard unsettled her, and after what seemed an age she averted her gaze to a point somewhere beyond his right shoulder.

'What about the next time he lays in wait for you?' Nikos queried relentlessly.

Michelle's eyes snapped back into focus. 'There won't *be* a next time.'

'You're so sure about that?'

'If there is, I can handle it,' she reiterated firmly.

'Such confidence.'

'I handled you.'

His smile lacked any pretense at humour. 'At no time did my motives stem from a desire to frighten or harm you.'

'I didn't know that.' Any more than she knew it now.

'No,' he qualified, and glimpsed the way her body jerked imperceptibly, and the defensive tightening of her arms as she sought to control it. He wasn't done, and he derived no satisfaction or pleasure in what he intended to say. 'Don't presume to judge the son by his parents.'

'Hidden messages, Nikos?' Her eyes were clear as they met his.

The unexpected peal of the telephone startled her.

'Aren't you going to answer that?'

She moved to the handset and picked up the receiver.

'Michelle.'

Jeremy. Her fingers tightened. 'I have nothing to say to you.' She hung up without giving him the opportunity to utter a further word.

A minute later it rang again, and she ignored it for several seconds before snatching the receiver.

'I'm sorry.' His voice was ragged, and came in quick bursts. 'I was jealous. I didn't mean to hurt you.'

She didn't bother answering, and simply replaced the receiver.

Within seconds the telephone rang again, and she caught up the receiver, only to have it taken out of her hand.

'Call once more, and I'll ensure Michelle notifies the police,' Nikos directed brusquely. The tirade of abuse that followed was ugly. 'What you're suggesting is anatomically impossible. However I'm quite prepared to get a legal opinion on it. Would you care for me to do that?'

It was obvious Jeremy didn't want anything of the kind, and she watched as Nikos replaced the receiver.

'Does he have a key to your apartment?'

'No.' Indignation rose to the fore, and erupted in angry speech. 'No, he doesn't. No one does.'

'I'm relieved to hear it.'

Michelle fixed him with a fulminating glare. 'What I do with my life and who I do it with is none of your business.'

He admired her spirit, and there was a part of him that wanted to pull her into his arms and hold her close. Except he knew if he so much as touched her, she'd scratch and claw like a cornered cat.

'Tonight I made it my business.'

'I didn't leave the Gallery until half an hour after everyone else,' Michelle flung at him. 'How come you happened to still be hanging around?'

'I was on foot, remember? I noticed Jeremy sitting in a car he made no attempt to start.'

Nikos didn't need to paint a word picture. She got it without any help at all, in techni-colour.

'I should thank you.'

His mouth tilted fractionally. 'So—thank me.'

Her eyes met his. 'I thought I just did.'

'And now you want me to leave.'

'Please.'

She watched as he extracted his wallet, withdrew a card, scrawled a series of digits and placed it onto the countertop.

'My mobile number. You can reach me on it anytime.'

She followed him from the kitchen, paused as he caught up his jacket, then crossed the lounge to the front door.

Nikos lifted a hand and brushed his fingers down her cheek. 'Goodnight, *kyria.*'

He didn't linger, and she told herself she was glad. She closed the door, set the locking mechanism in place, and threw the bolt.

Then she crossed to a comfortable chair and activated the remote.

Cable television provided endless choices, and she stared resolutely at the screen in an effort to block out what had transpired in the past hour.

She focused on the Gallery, its success, Emilio, until it became increasingly difficult to keep her eyes open, then she simply closed them, uncaring where she slept.

CHAPTER FIVE

MICHELLE woke at dawn to the sound of male voices and lifted her head in alarm, only to subside as realisation affirmed the television was on and the voice belonged to actor Don Johnson as Sonny in a rerun of 'Miami Vice.'

Her limbs felt stiff, and she stretched in an effort to ease them, then she checked her watch.

There was time for a swim in the indoor pool, then she'd shower and change, grab some breakfast, and drive to the Gallery.

It was almost nine when she swung the Porsche into a parking bay, and she used her key to unlock the outer Gallery door.

'*Buon giorno.*'

'Hi,' she greeted, and cast Emilio an appreciative smile as she saw the fruits of his labour in highly polished floors and everything restored to immaculate order. 'You're an angel.'

'Ah, from you that is indeed a compliment.'

'I mean it.'

The corners of his eyes crinkled with humour, and his smile was warm and generous. 'I know you do.'

'As you've cleaned up, I'll do the book work, enter the accounts, make the phone calls.'

'But first, the coffee.' He moved towards her and caught hold of her shoulders, then frowned as he saw her wince. His eyes narrowed as he glimpsed the shadows beneath her eyes. 'Headache, no sleep, what?'

'A bit of all three.'

She bore his scrutiny with equanimity. 'Elaborate on the *what*, Michelle.'

Emilio called her *darling, honey, cara,* but rarely *Michelle*.

'It was such a successful evening,' she prevaricated.

'Uh-huh,' he disclaimed. 'We've achieved other successful evenings, none of which have seen you pale, wan, and hollow-eyed the next morning.'

She opted to go for the truth. Or as much of it as he needed to know. 'I watched a film on cable, then fell asleep in the lounge.' She arched her neck, and rolled her head a little. 'I'm a little stiff, that's all.'

He didn't say anything for several long seconds. 'Nice try, *cara.*'

'You mentioned coffee?'

Michelle took hers into the office, and set to work entering details from yesterday's sales into the computer. She double-checked the receipts and entries before printing out the accounts, then stacked them in alphabetical order. A few of their regular clientele had paid by personal cheque, and she organised the banking deposit sheet.

She made telephone calls and arranged packing and delivery, then checked with the clientele to ascertain if the times quoted were convenient.

When the intercom beeped, she activated it. 'Yes, Emilio?'

'Jeremy Bateson-Burrows is here. Shall I send him in?'

'No.' Her refusal was swift, and she breathed in deeply before qualifying, 'I don't want to see him.'

A minute later the intercom beeped again. 'He says it's of vital importance.'

Michelle cursed beneath her breath. 'Tell him I'll be down in a minute.'

Her stiletto heels made a clicking noise on the polished floor, and she saw Jeremy turn towards her as she drew close.

Emilio was within sight some distance away arranging a display of decorative ceramic urns.

'Jeremy,' she greeted with cool formality.

'I wanted to apologise in person.'

Careful, an inner voice cautioned. 'It's a little too late for that,' she said evenly. 'If you'll excuse me, I have a considerable amount of work to get through.'

'I need to talk to you, to explain. Have lunch with me. Please?' He was very convincing. Too convincing. 'I don't know what came over me last night,' he said desperately.

'I'd like you to leave. Now,' Michelle said quietly.

He reached out a hand as if to touch her arm, and she stepped back a few paces.

'Michelle.'

Emilio's intrusion was heaven-sent, and she turned towards him in silent query.

'I'm in the middle of an international call,' Emilio announced smoothly. 'Nikos Alessandros has arrived to arrange delivery and payment. Can you attend to him?'

He held the mobile phone, and she almost believed him until she glimpsed the dark stillness apparent in his expression.

'Yes, of course.'

Nikos watched as she walked towards him, and controlled the brief surge of anger as she drew close. She looked as fragile as the finest glass.

'Good morning.' Or was it afternoon? Hell, she'd lost track of whether it was one or the other.

His eyes met hers, dark, analytical, unwavering, and her eyes widened slightly as he leaned forward and cupped her face with both hands.

His mouth covered hers with a gentleness that made the breath catch in her throat, and she was unable to suppress the shivery sensation scudding down her spine as his tongue softly explored the delicate tissues, slowly traced each abrasion, then tangled briefly with her tongue before withdrawing.

He let both hands drop to his side, then he circled her waist and drew her close.

'What's going on? Michelle?' Jeremy's voice was hard and filled with querulous anger.

Nikos' arm tightened fractionally in silent warning, and the look he cast down at her was warm and incredibly intimate. 'I don't see the need to keep it a secret, do you?' He shifted his attention to Emilio. 'Michelle and I have decided to resume our relationship.'

She heard the words, assimilated them, and didn't have a chance to draw breath as Nikos soundly kissed her.

Why did she have the feeling she was one of three players on a stage, with an audience of only one? Because that was the precise scenario, and it came as no surprise when Jeremy brushed past them and exited the Gallery.

Emilio locked the door after him and turned the ''open'' sign round to read ''closed.''

'You can't do that,' Michelle protested.

'I just did. So what are you going to do about it?' Emilio queried lightly, adding in jest—'Sue me?'

She looked from one to the other, then fixed her gaze on Nikos. 'You've really put the fat in the fire now.' Reaction began to rear its head. 'Do you realise the news will probably reach my parents? What will they think?' She closed her eyes, then opened them again in the knowledge that her darling *maman* would undoubtedly be delighted. Another thought rose to the fore, and her expression became fierce. 'This situation plays right into your hands with Saska, doesn't it?'

'Who is Saska?' Emilio asked with interest, and Nikos informed him urbanely.

'The recently widowed wife of a very close friend.'

'Whom Nikos suggested I collaborate with him to deceive,' Michelle added.

'Ah,' Emilio commented with a shrug in comprehension. 'But you wouldn't play, huh?'

'No, she wouldn't,' Nikos said smoothly.

A wide smile showed white teeth and lent dark eyes a lively sparkle. 'I think you should, *cara.* Play,' Emilio added quizzically. 'It would do you good.'

'Emilio,' Michelle warned. 'I don't find this in the least amusing.'

'No, darling, I don't expect you do.' His expression sobered slightly. Jeremy was the catalyst, and Nikos, unless he was mistaken, was a man with a hidden agenda. 'You'll forgive me if I say I shall enjoy the show?' He didn't give her the opportunity to respond.

'I don't need to tell you that your secret is safe with me. Now, why don't you go have lunch together, and fine tune your strategy?'

'Yes,' Nikos agreed. 'Why don't we do that?'

She cast him a discerning look, opened her mouth to argue, then closed it again. 'I'll get my bag.' She crossed to the office, retrieved it, then swung back to the entrance.

Emilio was talking into the mobile phone, and she fluttered her fingers at him, checked her watch, and silently indicated she'd be back at two.

'I suggest somewhere close by in air-conditioned comfort,' Nikos indicated silkily as they walked into the midsummer sunshine.

Michelle slid down her sunglasses, and was aware he mirrored her actions. 'Fine. You choose.'

Ten minutes later they were seated in seclusion at a table overlooking an outdoor courtyard filled with potted flowers and greenery plants of numerous description.

'Your parents have invited Saska to their home this evening.'

Michelle looked at him over the rim of her glass. He looked relaxed and at ease, and far too compelling for his own good. '*Maman* is the consummate hostess,' she said evenly. 'I'm sure you'll both enjoy yourselves.'

She replaced the glass as the waiter delivered their order.

'I'll collect you at five to six.'

'I have other plans.'

'Change them.'

'Those plans involve other people. I don't want to let them down at such short notice.'

His eyes speared hers. 'I'm sure they'll understand if you explain.'

Yes they would, but that wasn't the point.

Michelle picked up her fork and stabbed a crouton, some cos lettuce, and regarded the poised fork with apparent interest. She was bargaining for time, and it irked that he knew. 'Surely the charade can wait a few days?'

'Antonia and Emerson Bateson-Burrows are fellow guests,' Nikos intimated. 'Won't they think it a little strange if you're not there?' He waited a beat. 'And Saska is seen to be my partner?'

She had to concede he had a point. 'I guess you're right.'

Why did she feel like she'd just made a life-changing decision? How long would this pretense need to last? A few weeks? A month? It wasn't as if they had to attend every party and dinner in town. It was likely she'd only have to see him a couple of nights a week.

Just keep your emotions intact, a tiny voice taunted.

Michelle took a sip of mineral water, then speared another morsel of food. The salad was delicious, but her appetite diminished with every mouthful.

What about the chemistry? The way she felt when he touched her? Each time he kissed her, whether in sensual exploration or passion, she'd just wanted to die.

Dear heaven, she'd experienced more emotional upheaval in the past two days than she had in...a long time, she admitted.

Nikos observed each fleeting expression, and wondered if she realised how expressive her features were? Or how easily he was able to define them?

'I guess we should set down some ground rules.' That sounded fair, she determined. How had Emilio put it? *Fine tune your strategy.*

'What did you have in mind?'

Michelle looked at him carefully, and was unable to see beyond the sophisticated mask he presented. Oh God, was she *mad?* She wasn't even in the same league, let alone the same game. So why was she choosing to play?

'You don't make decisions for me, and vice versa,' she began. 'We consult on anything that involves the both of us.'

'That's reasonable.'

So far, so good. 'No unnecessary—' She was going to say *intimacy,* but that sounded too personal. 'Touching,' she amended, and missed the faint gleam in those dark eyes.

'I'll try to restrain myself, if you will.'

He was amused, damn him! 'This isn't funny,' she reproved, and he proffered a crooked smile.

'My sense of humour got the better of me.'

'Do you want to put a time limit on this?'

One eyebrow slanted. 'Lunch?'

'Our supposed relationship!'

'Ah—that.' He expertly wound the last of his fettuccine onto his fork and savoured it. 'How about…as long as it takes?'

Of course. That was the entire object of the exercise. She'd had enough salad, and she pushed the bowl forward, then sank back in her chair.

'I'm intrigued,' she ventured. 'To discover how you knew I'd studied at the Sorbonne?'

He looked at her carefully. 'I endeavour to discover background details of the people who claim to want to do business with me. It's a precautionary measure.'

Michelle's eyes narrowed slightly. That meant being able to access confidential data on file. Although with the right contacts and connections, it wouldn't be difficult.

'Emerson Bateson-Burrows has been vigilant in baiting the figurative hook,' Nikos revealed with wry cynicism.

As her parents mixed socially with Jeremy's parents, they, too, had come beneath Nikos' scrutiny. It didn't leave her with a comfortable feeling.

'We didn't meet in Paris.'

'Yes, we did,' he corrected.

'Where?' she demanded. 'I would have remembered.'

'At a party.'

It was possible. She'd attended several parties during her Paris sojourn. Although she was positive she'd never seen Nikos Alessandros at any one of them. 'We weren't introduced,' she said with certainty.

'No,' Nikos agreed. 'It was a case of too many people, and I was with someone else.'

Now why did that suddenly make her feel jealous? It didn't make sense.

'You'd better let me have your phone number in case I need to contact you,' he said smoothly, and she lifted one eyebrow in mocking query.

'You mean you don't already have it?'

His gaze was steady. 'I'd prefer you to give it to me willingly.'

She looked at him for a second, then she reached into her bag, extracted a card and handed it to him.

'Would you like something else to eat?' When she shook her head, he indicated, 'Dessert? Coffee?'

How long had they been here? Half an hour? Longer? 'No. Thanks,' she added. 'I have a few things to do before I go back to the Gallery.' She didn't, but Nikos wasn't to know that. 'Would you excuse me?'

He lifted one hand, gained the attention of the waiter, and rose to his feet. 'I'll walk back with you.'

She opened her mouth to say 'there's no need,' saw his expression, and decided to refrain from saying anything at all.

Nikos signed the proffered credit slip, pocketed the duplicate, then accompanied her onto the street.

Finding 'things to do' didn't stretch her imagination, and she made the bakery first on her list, where she selected bread rolls, a couple of Danish pastries. For Emilio, she justified. To lend credence, she entered the small local post office and stood in line to buy stamps.

Did Nikos suspect her mission was a sham? Possibly. But she didn't care.

'Are you done?'

The sound of that soft slightly accented drawl merely added encouragement, and she stepped into the pharmacy, picked up some antiseptic liquid, paid for it, then emerged onto the pavement.

The fruit shop was next, and she selected some grapes, an apple, a banana, and two tomatoes, justifying her purchases, 'I won't have time to get anything after work.'

It took only minutes to reach the Gallery, but they were long minutes during which she was acutely conscious of his height and breadth as he walked at her side.

Twice she thought of something to say by way of conversation only to dismiss the words as being inane.

At the Gallery entrance she paused and thanked him for lunch, then looked askance as he followed her inside.

'If you remember there was a distraction,' Nikos reminded indolently. 'I need to give you a cheque, and have you arrange delivery.'

Michelle tended to it with professional efficiency, then accompanied him to the door.

'What have we here?' Emilio queried, indicating her purchases shortly after Nikos' departure.

'Things.' She selected the bakery bag and handed it to him. 'For you.'

His soft laughter was almost her undoing. 'You initiated a small diversion?'

'Minor,' she agreed, and he shook his head in silent chastisement.

'Tonight could prove interesting.'

Michelle merely smiled and headed towards the office.

It was after five when she parked her car in its allotted space and rode the lift to her apartment.

The message light was blinking on the answering machine, and she activated the 'message' button, listened to Jeremy's voice as he issued an impassioned plea to call him, deliberated all of five seconds, then hit 'erase.'

His increasingly obsessive behaviour disturbed her, and she stood in reflective silence, aware that at no time had she given him reason to believe they could share anything more than friendship.

A quick glance at her watch revealed she had half an hour in which to shower and dress before she was due to meet Nikos downstairs.

Michelle entered the lobby as Nikos' BMW swept into the bricked apron immediately adjacent the main entrance, and she reached the car just as he emerged from behind the wheel.

Nikos noted the slight thrust of her chin, the cool expressive features, and suppressed a faint smile at the sleek upswept hairstyle. The make-up was perfection with clever emphasis on her eyes, the generous curve of her mouth.

The classic "little black dress" had a scooped neckline, very short sleeves and a hemline that stopped mid-thigh, with high stiletto-heeled black pumps accenting the length of her legs.

Everything about her enhanced the sophisticated image of a young woman in total control.

Michelle slid into the passenger seat and offered him a faint smile in greeting.

He looked relaxed, and she wished she could feel comfortable about deceiving her parents.

The car gained clear passage onto the road, and Nikos headed towards the main arterial road leading into Surfers Paradise.

'Ten minutes to countdown.'

'Less,' Nikos declared. 'It begins when we collect Saska from her hotel.'

Within minutes he drew the car to a halt adjacent the Marriott. 'I won't be long.'

She watched as he disappeared through the automatic glass doors, crossed to one of several armchairs in the large lobby, and greeted a tall elegantly dressed woman.

Beautiful wasn't an adequate description, Michelle decided as Nikos escorted the brunette to the car.

The mental image Michelle had drawn of a depressed and desperately unhappy widow didn't fit the vital young woman who conversed with ease during the ten-minute drive to Sovereign Islands, a group of seven man-made residential islands situated three kilometres north, and reached by an overbridge from the mainland.

Chantelle and Etienne Gerard's home was a modern architectural tri-level home, with two levels given over entirely to entertaining.

There were several cars lining the driveway, and Michelle experienced a vague sense of uneasiness as she entered the house at Nikos' side. She was all too aware of the role she'd committed herself to play and the deceit involved.

Almost on cue, Nikos caught hold of her hand and linked his fingers through her own, and the smile he cast her was intimately warm.

It stirred her senses and made her acutely aware of each breath she took. The blood seemed to race through her veins, quickening her pulse.

Oh God. What had she let herself in for?

CHAPTER SIX

'Nikos, Saska, how nice to see you.' Chantelle, ever the gracious hostess, greeted them with pleasant enthusiasm, then she leaned forward and touched her daughter's cheek with her own. 'Darling, I'm so pleased you could come.'

Her mother's 'just a few friends' extended to more than thirty, Michelle estimated as Chantelle led them through the house and out onto the large terrace overlooking a wide canal.

Hired staff were in evidence to ensure trays of finger food and drinks were constantly on offer.

Introductions and greetings were exchanged with the ease of long practice as they mingled with fellow guests.

Every now and then she felt the pressure of Nikos' fingers on her own, and several times she made a furtive attempt to free them without success.

Antonia and Emerson Bateson-Burrows were among the guests, and Michelle's stomach twisted a little at the thought that Jeremy might put in an appearance.

'Have you known Nikos for long?'

Was this a trick question? Surely Nikos had already provided Saska with *some* basic information?

'We met while Michelle was studying in Paris,' Nikos answered for her, and Michelle wrinkled her nose at him.

'Really, darling,' she chastised teasingly. 'I'm quite capable of answering for myself.' She turned towards Saska and rolled her eyes. 'At a party.' Surely it would do no harm to elaborate a little? 'Five years ago.' That fit in well. 'I was a student with a very new Arts degree, which my parents agreed should be followed by a year at the Sorbonne.' She lifted her shoulders in a typically Gaelic shrug. 'Intense study, you know how it is. I was dragged off to a party with friends. Nikos was there.'

Saska's eyes assumed a faintly quizzical gleam. 'Alone?'

'Of course not.' This could almost be fun, meshing fact with fiction. 'His companion for the evening was a stunning blonde.'

'He was obviously attracted to you.'

'Very much so,' Nikos admitted as he carried Michelle's hand to his lips, and she felt the graze of teeth against her knuckles in silent warning.

Which she took delight in ignoring. 'He played the gentleman, and was very circumspect in his interest.' She met his gaze and openly dared him to refute her words. 'Weren't you, darling?'

'Until the next time.'

The *knowledge* was there, apparent, and acted as a subtle reminder that when it came to game-playing, he was more than her equal.

'Michelle. Nikos.'

It was a relief to have Emilio join them, and she cast him a generous smile as Nikos introduced Saska.

'Pleasant evening,' Emilio commented, switching his attention to the widowed brunette. 'You're here on holiday?'

'Yes. Nikos suggested I take a break for a few weeks.'

'Perhaps we could have dinner together one night soon? Tuesday?'

My, Emilio was moving quickly, Michelle acknowledged silently, watching as Saska effected a slight lift of her shoulders.

'If that is acceptable to Nikos and Michelle?'

Whoa. A foursome? *Tomorrow?*

'We'll be delighted, won't we, *pedhi mou?*'

The endearment was deliberate, and she was tempted to say *no,* but knew it would sound churlish. 'Delighted,' she agreed. At the first opportunity, she decided, she would have words with Nikos about the frequency of such 'dates.'

Michelle took another sip of excellent champagne and removed a seafood savoury from a proffered tray. It seemed hours since she'd picked at a salad over lunch.

'What a magnificent view,' Saska enthused as she gazed out over the water. 'Nikos, you must tell me the history behind the design of these islands.'

'Take Saska down onto the jetty,' Michelle directed, and felt a tingle of pleasure at thwarting him. 'It's possible to obtain a more effective view from there.'

This was not part of the plan. It was evident from the faint warning flare in the depths of those eyes.

'Michelle is more knowledgeable,' he responded smoothly.

It was a very neat manoeuvre, and one she couldn't really extricate herself from without appearing impolite.

The ground was landscaped on three terraced levels from the outdoor pool down to the water's edge. Lavish landscaping included concrete steps, a decorative rockery, a large fountain, flower-edged paths, and expanses of lush green lawn.

Michelle led the way, and when they reached the jetty she stepped out to its furthest point as she directed Saska's attention towards the Broadwater.

'The stretch of land immediately in front of us is known as south Stradbroke Island. Beyond it lays the Pacific Ocean.'

Saska leaned forward. 'And these islands?'

'Manmade. Each small island is connected to the other by a series of bridges. It's very effective, don't you think?'

Saska didn't speak for several minutes. 'Nikos is a special friend,' she relayed conversationally. 'We've known each other a long time.'

Michelle didn't pretend not to understand. 'I imagine there's a purpose to you telling me this?'

'I find it unusual he has never mentioned you.'

Why did she suddenly feel as if she'd just stepped into a minefield? 'As you know, Nikos has diverse business interests in many European cities.' She was plucking reasons out of nowhere. 'We met not long before I was due to return to Australia to discover my niche in the art world.' A small elaboration, but much of it had its base in truth.

'And now?' Saska persisted. 'I understand you've only recently rediscovered each other?'

'Yes.'

'Do you love him?'

Think, she directed mentally. You can hardly say *no.* 'I care,' she said simply, and added for good measure, 'Very much.' May the heavens not descend on her head for such a transgression!

'So do I,' the brunette declared.

'What are you advocating? Swords drawn at dawn, and a fight to the death?'

Saska smiled, then began to laugh, and the effect transformed her features into something of rare beauty. 'I like you.'

'Well now,' Michelle drawled. 'That's a bonus.'

'In fact,' Saska deliberated. 'I think you'd be very good for Nikos.' The smile widened. 'But then, so would I. We share the same heritage, the same interests, the same friends. As much as I grieve for my dead husband, I have discovered I do not like being alone. Do we understand one another?'

'Yes. But haven't you neglected the most important factor?'

Saska lifted a finely arched eyebrow. 'I don't think so.'

'Nikos. The choice is his to make, don't you think?'

'Of course.'

Confidence was a fine thing. 'Now we've had this little chat,' Michelle said evenly, 'shall we rejoin the other guests?'

'By all means.'

The evening air was still, and although light, there was a hint of impending dusk as shadows began to lengthen. The water lost its deep blue and began to acquire a shade of grey as the colours lost their sharp intensity.

Numerous garden lights sprang on, together with lit columns around the pool, illuminating the terrace and surrounding area.

Nikos moved forward to meet them, and although his smile encompassed both women, his hand settled in the small of Michelle's back for an instant before his fingers began a soothing movement up and down the indentations of her spine.

It felt warm, electric, and did crazy things to her composure. A sensation that was heightened when he leaned towards her and brushed his lips close to her ear before proffering her a plate of food.

It was then she caught sight of Jeremy, and her appetite became non-existent.

'I thought you might be hungry.'

'Not really.'

He picked up a savoury and held it tempt-ingly close to her mouth. 'Try this.' When she shook her head, he took a small bite and offered her the rest.

What was he doing, for heaven's sake? She took the savoury from his fingers and ate it, then looked at him in exasperation when he followed it with another. 'Isn't this overkill?'

'You could at least look as if you're en-joying it.' His voice was pure silk, and she retaliated by biting more deeply than neces-sary, caught his finger with her teeth as she intended, then managed to look incredibly contrite. 'Oh darling, did I bite you? I'm so sorry.'

'I think I'll live.'

'Perhaps you could get me a drink?'

'Champagne?'

She deliberated for all of five seconds. 'Of course.' Not a wise choice, but she'd sip it slowly for a while, then discard it in favour of mineral water.

'Saska?'

All he had to do was catch the waiter's attention, and seconds later their drinks were delivered. Nikos possessed a certain air of command that drew notice. Add a compelling degree of power with sophisticated élan, and the combination was lethal.

Her eyes were drawn to those strong sculpted features, the broad facial bone structure, the well-defined jaw, and the firm lines of his mouth.

What would he be like if ever he lost control? A faint shiver slithered its way over the surface of her skin. Devastating, a tiny voice prompted. Unbridled, flagrant, *primitive*.

At that moment his eyes met hers, and held. Her own dilated, and she felt as if her breath became suspended. Then his lips curved to form a lazy smile that held knowledge and a sense of pleasurable anticipation.

He couldn't *see* what she was thinking…could he? And it wasn't as if she *wanted* to go to bed with him. Heaven forbid! That would be akin to selling her soul.

Besides, you might never recover, a secret inner voice taunted.

She'd seen women who never experienced their sexual equal prowl the party circuit in search of an adequate replacement. They tended to possess few scruples, dressed to kill, and drank a little too much.

She needed to get away for a few minutes, and the powder room provided an excellent reason. 'If you'll excuse me?' She handed her champagne flute to Nikos. 'I won't be long.'

Michelle paused several times en route to extend a greeting to a number of her parents' friends. Indoors there were two guests lingering adjacent the powder room, and she bypassed them and headed for the curved flight of stairs leading to the upper floor which housed her parents' suite and no less than five guest rooms with en suite facilities.

She chose one, then lingered to tidy her hair and retouch her lipstick.

Michelle emerged into the bedroom, and came to a shocked standstill at the sight of Jeremy leaning against the doorjamb.

'These are my parents' private quarters,' she managed evenly.

She kept walking, hoping he would move aside and allow her to pass. He didn't, and she paused a few feet in front of him. 'Jeremy, you're blocking my way.'

Her instincts were on alert. However, the upper floor was well insulated from the people and noise on the terrace out back of the house. Even if she screamed, it was doubtful anyone would hear a thing.

She took a step forward only to have him catch hold of her arm.

'Wasn't I good enough?' Jeremy demanded softly.

'Your father and mine are business associates,' she said carefully. 'Our parents share a similar social circle. We were friends,' she added.

'You're saying that's all it was?'

'For me, yes.' She looked at him, glimpsed the darkness apparent in his eyes, and knew she'd need to tread carefully. 'I'm sorry if you thought it was more than friendship.'

'If Nikos hadn't put in an appearance that night...' He trailed to a halt.

She was silent for several long seconds. 'It wouldn't have made any difference.'

'That's not true,' he said fiercely. 'You have to give me another chance.'

Not in this lifetime. She chose not to say a word.

'Michelle!' The plea was impassioned, and desperate. Too desperate.

'What do you hope to achieve by holding me here?' She had to keep talking. And pray someone, *Nikos,* would think it curious she'd been away so long and investigate.

His face contorted. 'Have you slept with him yet?'

'You don't have the right to ask that.'

'Damn you. I'm making it my right.' He yanked her close up against him, twisted her arm behind her back and thrust a hand between her thighs. His fingers were a vicious instrument for all of ten seconds before she went for the bridge of his nose, but he ducked and the side of her palm connected with his cheekbone.

'I doubt Nikos will want you when he knows I've had you first.'

All of a sudden she was free, and Jeremy lay groaning on the carpet.

'You won't have the opportunity.' Nikos' voice held the chill of an arctic floe. 'A restraining order will be put into effect immediately. If you violate it, you'll be arrested and charged.'

Nikos swept her a swift encompassing glance, and his eyes darkened as he took in her waxen features, the way her fingers shook as they smoothed over her hair.

'You can't have me arrested,' Jeremy flung wildly as he scrambled to his feet, and Michelle almost quaked at the controlled savagery evident in Nikos' response.

'Watch me.'

'My father—'

'Doesn't have enough money to get you out of this one. Attempted rape is a serious charge.'

Jeremy's face reddened, and he blustered—'I didn't touch her.'

Nikos reached out a hand and sought purchase on Jeremy's jacket.

'What are you doing?'

'Detaining you while Michelle fetches your parents.'

'Everything comes with a price. My father will pay yours.'

'As he has in the past?' Nikos queried silkily. 'Not this time,' he stated with a finality that moved Jeremy close to hysteria as Michelle stepped through the doorway.

'Don't bring my mother. She'd never understand.'

'Then perhaps it's time she did,' Nikos said pitilessly.

'Michelle, don't,' Jeremy begged. 'I'll do anything you want. I promise.'

'We can do this one of two ways. Michelle fetches your parents and you're removed from these premises without fuss. Or I force you downstairs and onto the terrace for a very public denouncement. Choose,' he commanded hardily.

Michelle smoothed a shaky hand over her hair in a purely reflex action as she descended the stairs. Reaction was beginning to set in, and she drew a deep breath in an effort to regain a measure of composure.

What followed wasn't something she would choose to experience again in a long time. Parental love was one thing. Blind maternal devotion was something else.

Nikos dismissed Emerson's bribe, and suggested the Bateson-Burrows remove their son as quickly as possible.

At which point Chantelle arrived on the scene, took everything in with a glance, and demanded an explanation.

'Jeremy has had a little too much to drink,' Emerson indicated smoothly. 'We're taking him home.'

As soon as they were alone Chantelle looked from Michelle to Nikos. 'Would one of you care to tell me what really happened here?'

Michelle didn't say a word.

'Nikos?'

'Jeremy failed to accept Michelle and I have a relationship.' His eyes were hard, his expression equally so. 'He hassled her last night when she left the Gallery, and tonight he went one step further.'

Chantelle looked suitably horrified. '*Cherie,* this is terrible. Are you all right?'

'I'm fine, *Maman,*' Michelle reassured her quietly.

'I'll see to it that Michelle initiates a restraining order. Jeremy has a history of violence,' Nikos informed grimly. 'One recorded offense in Sydney three years ago.'

'The Bateson-Burrows moved to the Coast almost three years ago,' Chantelle reflected slowly.

'He was expelled from two private schools, and kicked out of University,' Nikos continued. 'In Perth, Adelaide, and Melbourne.'

Chantelle straightened her shoulders. She didn't ask how he acquired the information. It was enough that he had. 'It's to be hoped they soon leave the Coast.'

'It appears to be a familiar pattern.'

'Meanwhile, Michelle—'

'Will stay with me.'

'Now just a minute,' Michelle intervened, and met his dark gaze.

'It's not negotiable, *pedhi mou*.'

'The hell it's not!'

'*Cherie,* for my sake, as well as your own, do as Nikos suggests. Please.'

'I'll tell Saska we're leaving early,' Nikos declared. 'If she wants to stay, she can get a taxi back to the hotel.'

'Can I get you something, darling?' Chantelle queried as soon as Nikos disappeared down the hallway. 'A drink? Some coffee? A brandy?'

'I'm OK. Really,' she assured in a bid to lessen her mother's anxiety. 'Just a bit shaken, that's all.'

'Antonia and Emerson—Jeremy. I had no idea,' she said wretchedly. 'Thank heavens Nikos was here.'

All this has happened *because* of Nikos, she felt like saying. Yet that wasn't entirely true. Nikos' presence had only accelerated Jeremy's irrational jealousy.

'Maman.' She paused, then changed her mind against confiding that her purported relationship with the powerful Greek was just a sham.

'Yes, darling?'

'I'll just go tidy up.' She felt the need to remove Jeremy's touch, preferably with a long very thorough soaping in the shower. But for now, she'd settle for pressing a cold flannel to her face and redoing her hair.

Nikos had returned by the time she emerged, and she met his swift gaze, held it, then she crossed to brush her lips to her mother's cheek.

'I'll ring you in the morning.'

Chantelle hugged her close, then reluctantly released her. 'Please. Take care.'

Minutes later Nikos eased the powerful BMW onto the road, and she didn't offer a word as he drove to Main Beach.

'I'll be fine on my own,' Michelle stated as he parked the car outside her apartment building and slid out from behind the wheel.

'Nice try.'

She faced him across the car roof, glimpsed the dark glittery look he cast her, and felt like stamping her foot in frustrated anger. 'Look—'

'Do you want to walk, or have me carry you?' Nikos' voice was hard, his intention inflexible.

'Go to hell!'

'I've been there. Twice in the past twenty-four hours. It's not something I plan to repeat.' He moved round the car to her side. 'Now, which way is it going to be?'

'If you dare—' Whatever else she planned to say was lost in a muffled sound as he simply hoisted her over one shoulder, walked to the entrance, activated the door with her security card, then strode towards the bank of lifts at the far end of the lobby.

'Put me down, dammit!' She beat fists against his back, aimed for his kidneys, and groaned in frustration when he shifted her out of range. A mean-intentioned kick failed to connect, and she growled as fiercely as a feline under attack as he gained the lift, punched the appropriate panel button, then when the lift stopped, he walked calmly to her apartment, unlocked the door, and only when they were inside did he let her slide down to her feet.

'You want to fight?' he challenged silkily. 'Go ahead.'

She wanted to, badly, and right at this precise moment she didn't care that she couldn't win.

'You,' she vented with ill-concealed fury. 'Are the most arrogant, egotistical man I've ever met. I want you to leave, now.'

'It's here,' Nikos stated ruthlessly. 'Or my apartment. Choose.'

Something about his stance, the stillness of his features slowly leeched most of the anger from her system.

'Don't you think you're taking the *hero* role too far?'

'No.'

Succinct, and clearly unmoveable. Maybe she should just concede defeat now and save her emotional and physical energy. It would be a whole lot easier than continuing to rage against him.

'I could ring the police and have them evict you.' It was a last-ditch effort, and she knew it.

'Go ahead.'

She badly wanted to call his bluff. Except she had no trouble visualising how such a scene would evolve, and how it would inevitably prove to be an exercise in futility.

Occasionally there could be success in conceding defeat. 'You can sleep in the spare room.'

She turned away from him and crossed the lounge to her bedroom and carefully closed the door.

If he insisted on staying—*fine*. She was going to have a long hot bath with bath oil and bubbles…the whole bit. Then when she was done, she'd dry off and climb into bed, hopefully to sleep until the alarm went off in the morning.

Michelle stayed in the scented water for a long time. It was bliss, absolute bliss to lay there and let the perfumed heat seep into her bones and soothe her mind.

It had a soporific effect, and she closed her eyes. For only a minute, she was prepared to swear, when a rapid knock on the door caused her to jackknife into a sitting position.

Seconds later the door opened and Nikos walked calmly into the bathroom.

'What the hell are you doing in here?'

She looked like a child, was his first thought, with her hair piled on top of her head, and all but buried beneath a layer of frothy foam.

'Checking you hadn't fallen asleep and drowned.'

Her eyes were huge, the pupils dilated with anger.

Most women would have sank back displaying most if not all of their breasts, and behaved like a sultry temptress by inviting him to join them.

'You could have waited for me to answer!'

'You didn't,' he relayed coolly. 'That's why I came in.'

'Well, you can just turn around and go out again!' Indignation brought pink colour to her cheeks, and she looked at him through stormy eyes. Then, in a totally unprecedented action, she did the unforgivable. She scooped up water and foam and threw it at him in a spontaneous action that surprised her almost as much as it did him.

Her aim was good, it drenched the front part of his shirt, and she watched in fascination as a patch of foam began to dissipate. Then she lifted her gaze to lock with his. And wished fervently that she hadn't, for what she glimpsed there made her feel terribly afraid.

There was strength of purpose, a knowledge that was entirely primitive. For a moment she thought he was going to reach forward and drag her out of the bath and into his arms.

It was uncanny, but she could almost feel his mouth on hers, savour the taste of him as he invaded the soft inner tissues and explored them with his tongue. Staking a possession that could only have one ending.

The breath caught in her throat, and for seemingly long seconds she wasn't capable of saying a word.

'You provoked me,' she managed at last.

'Is that an apology?' Nikos demanded silkily.

'An explanation.'

His eyes speared hers. 'Pull the plug, and
get out of the bath.'

She looked at him incredulously. 'While
you're still here? Not on your life!'

He reached out, collected a large bath
towel, unfolded it and held it out.

Nikos saw the anger drain out of her. Her
eyes slowly welled, leaving them looking like
drenched pools. It twisted his gut, and undid
him more than anything she could have said.
Without a word he replaced the towel, then
he turned and walked from the en suite.

Michelle released the bath water, towelled
herself dry, then she pulled on a huge cotton
T-shirt and slid into bed to sit hugging her
knees as she stared sightlessly at a print positioned on the opposite wall.

The events of the past few hours played
and replayed through her mind until she
made a concerted effort to dismiss them.

Where was Nikos? Ensconced in the spare bedroom, or had he left the apartment?

She had no way of knowing, and told herself she didn't care. Except she had a vivid memory of the way her body reacted to his; the protective splay of his hand at her back; the intense warmth in his eyes when he looked at her. The feel of his mouth on hers, the way he invaded her senses and stirred them as no man had ever done before.

Michelle shifted position, picked up a book from the pedestal and read for a while. Three nights ago she'd been so engrossed in the plot she hadn't been able to put the book down. Now, she skimmed sentences and turned pages, only to discard it with disgust at her inability to focus on the plot.

All she needed, she determined as she switched off the light, was a good night's sleep.

CHAPTER SEVEN

MICHELLE woke with a start, the images so vivid for the space of a few seconds that she was prepared to swear they were real.

Jeremy, maniacal. Nikos, dark and threatening.

It was as if she was a disembodied spectator, watching the clash of steel as they fought, the thrust and parry as they each meshed their skill with physical prowess.

Then there was darkness, and she heard a cry of pain, followed by silence. She tried to ascertain who was the victor, but his features eluded her.

'Dear heaven,' Michelle whispered as she shifted into a sitting position and switched on the bedlamp. Light flooded the room, and she relished the reality of familiar surroundings.

Then she lifted her hands to her cheeks and discovered they were wet.

She scrubbed them dry, then she slid out of bed, pulled on a wrap, and walked quietly out to the kitchen. The digital display on the microwave relayed the time as one-o-five.

A cold drink would quench her thirst, and she selected a can, popped the top, and carried it into the lounge.

The night was warm, and she had an urge to slide open the wide glass doors and let the fresh sea air blow away the cares of the past few days.

Michelle stepped out onto the terrace and felt the coolness wash over her face. There was the tang of salt, a clean sweetness that drifted in from the ocean, and she breathed deeply as she took in the sweeping coastal view.

Street lamps, bright splashes of neon, pinpricks of light that diminished with distance from enumerable high-rise apartment buildings lining the coastal strip.

It resembled a fairyland of light against the velvet backdrop of an indigo night sky and ocean.

She lifted the can and took a long swallow of cool liquid. The breeze teased loose a few stray tendrils of hair and pulled at the hem of her wrap.

It could have been ten minutes or twenty before she returned indoors, and the sight of a tall male figure framed in the lounge brought her to a shocked standstill.

Her rational mind assured it was Nikos, but just for a split second with the reflected hall light behind him, her imagination went into overdrive.

'How long have you been standing there?' Was that her voice, sounding slightly high and vaguely breathless?

'Only a few minutes,' Nikos ventured quietly.

A towel was draped low on his hips, his chest and legs bare. It occurred that she hadn't even bothered to consider he wouldn't have anything to change into.

'I noticed the hall light go on half an hour ago.'

'So you decided to investigate.' She didn't mean to sound defensive. Except he could have no idea how vulnerable she was feeling right now, or be aware of the image he presented.

For one crazy moment she wanted to walk up to him and take comfort from the warmth of his embrace. Yet that was a madness she couldn't afford.

'I didn't mean to frighten you.'

Hadn't he been able to sleep? Or did he simply wake at the slightest sound? His features were dark, and in this half-light it was difficult to read his expression.

Her senses leapt at the electric energy apparent. It was almost as if all her fine body hairs rose up in anticipation of his touch, and she felt her heart quicken to a faster beat.

Get out of here, *now,* a tiny voice urged. Except her legs wouldn't obey the dictates of her brain.

The slow ache of desire flared deep inside, and she was aware of her shallow breathing, the pulse throbbing at the base of her throat.

Nikos didn't say a word as he took the few steps necessary to reach her, and his eyes held hers, compelling, dramatic, unwavering. Dark onyx fused with emerald, and she was unable to look away.

A hand closed over her shoulder, while the other slid beneath the heavy knot of her hair, loosened it, then when it fell to her shoulders he threaded his fingers through its length and smoothed a few stray tendrils behind her ear.

She felt him move imperceptibly, then sensed his lips brush over her hair and settle at the edge of one temple.

Unbidden she linked her arms round his waist and sank into him. She didn't want to think, she just wanted to feel. To become lost in sensation, transported to a place where there was only the moment, the man, and the passion.

She lifted her face to his, and felt the soft trail of kisses feather across her cheek, then descend to the generous curve of her mouth, tantalising, teasing, nibbling as he explored the soft fullness of her lower lip, tracing it with the tip of his tongue before delving in to make slow sweeping forays of the sweetness within.

It wasn't enough, not nearly enough, and she opened her mouth to him, angling her head in surrender as passion swept her to new heights.

Michelle dragged his mouth down to hers as his hand slid to her thigh and slowly crept up to her bottom, shaped it, then pressed her in close so she could be in no doubt of his arousal.

'Put your arms round my neck,' Nikos instructed, and she obeyed, only to catch her breath as he lifted her up against him and curved each thigh round his waist so that she straddled him.

Then he walked towards the bedroom, every step providing an erotic movement that heightened the ache deep inside.

She wanted, needed the physical joining, the hard thrusting primal rhythm as he took her with him to a place where there was only acute primitive sensation. Michelle was dimly aware they reached the bed. She felt him pause as he tossed back the bedcovers and drew her down onto the percale sheet, stilling as his eyes locked with hers.

He saw slumberous passion, desire, and something else that gave him pause. It would be so easy to take her, to sink into those moist depths and slake a mutual need until they reached satiation.

Instead he took the slow route, the long sensual tease that began with a sensory exploration of all her pleasure pulses, the sensitive crevices, as he used his lips, the soft pads of his fingers to touch and tantalise.

Michelle was unaware of the slight sounds she made deep in her throat as he took the tender peak of her breast into his mouth and began to shamelessly suckle until she cried out for him to desist. Then he merely shifted to its twin and brought her to the edge of pain.

Not content he caressed a path to her navel, explored it, then travelled low over her belly, teased the dark blonde curls with his tongue, then indulged in an intimacy that took her to the brink, then tipped her over the edge in a free fall that had her threshing against him, imploring him to stop…to never stop.

For one wild moment, she didn't think she could handle the intensity, then mercifully it began to ease, and she met his kiss hungrily, her hands eager, searching, wanting to bestow some of the pleasure he had gifted her.

She cried out as he caught her hands together and pressed them to his lips. There were a few emotive seconds as he paused to use prophylactic protection, then he positioned his length and eased into her, exulting in the gradual feeling of total enclosure as he slid deep. And stayed there for several long seconds before repeating the action. Longer and deeper, then harder and faster until she cried out and fell off the edge of the world.

What followed became a feast of the senses as he soothed her fevered flesh with a gentleness that brought her close to tears. He explored each sensitive pulse, felt her quivering response and savoured it in a long afterplay that stirred her senses to a point where it no longer became possible to lay supine, a willing supplicant to everything he chose to bestow.

She wanted to stir him to passion, to render him mindless beneath her touch until he begged her to stop.

With one easy movement she dragged herself free, then she captured his head between her hands and kissed him, thoroughly, slaking a sensual thirst as she employed sufficient pressure to roll him onto his back.

His eyes were dark, slumberous, and intent as she straddled his waist, then she trailed an exploratory path along one collarbone with her lips, dipped into the faint hollows, using her teeth to tease the hair on his chest, nibbling, savouring, tasting, until she reached one hard brown male nipple.

With extreme delicacy she laved it with her tongue and slowly suckled until the peak began to swell, then she took it between her teeth and employed the lightest pressure.

She felt, rather that heard his slight intake of breath, and she rolled the slightly distended peak with her teeth, then suckled with greedy sensitivity, all too aware of his fingers lightly brushing the soft fullness of her breasts.

Not content, she trailed a path of lingering kisses across his chest to bestow a similar treatment to its twin, and was unprepared for the sharp arrow that was part pleasure part pain as he took her nipple between two fingers and rolled it.

She gently swatted his hand and slid slowly down his torso, caressing the line of dark hair until she reached his stomach, hovered there for long tantalising seconds, then descended with such painstaking slowness.

Nikos held his breath as she began to explore with such devastating gentleness, it took all his willpower not to haul her into his arms and take control.

Yet he'd tested the measure of her endurance with an equally lingering sensual torture.

Nevertheless when she touched him lightly with the tip of her tongue, the breath hissed between his teeth, and her tentative examination brought a surge of powerful emotion. Not for the degree of her expertise. It was her touch, the desire to please him as he had pleasured her that brought him to the brink of climax.

Did she know she had this effect on a man? On *him?* Somehow he doubted it.

When he was almost ready to take independent action, she rose up in one graceful movement, carefully positioned herself, then slid slowly down until he was buried deep inside her.

It felt good, so very good. As if every nerve fibre, every sensory cell heightened as she sheathed and held him tightly.

There was a part of her that didn't want to move, simply to be. Yet there was a primal need for sensory stimulation, and she placed a hand on either side of his shoulders, then began to withdraw. Just a little, increasing the action until it became something primitive, and she cried out as his hands curved into her waist, held her still, then assumed the position of supremacy, lifting her high as his hips rose and fell endlessly until it was she who cried out, she who clutched hold of him.

Afterwards he held her, his fingers drifting a lazy pattern back and forth along her spine until her breathing quietened.

Michelle felt his lips graze her ear, then slip to the sensitive curve of her neck, linger there, before moving to the edge of her mouth.

His kiss was incredibly soft, the lightest touch as he savoured a path over the fullness of her lower lip.

'We're still—'

'Connected.'

She felt his mouth part in a humorous smile. 'Uncomfortable?'

'No.' The sound sighed from her lips. She felt as if she could lay here forever, absorbing the man, his texture and taste.

There were words she wanted to say. Words that would adequately express what she'd just experienced. How special it had been. Emotionally, spiritually, physically. For the first time she knew what it was like to be a part of someone on every level. To share, possess, and be possessed.

Frightening. For inevitably there would follow a sense of loss. *Don't think about it,* she bade silently. Just enjoy the night, and forget about what the new day might bring.

It wasn't love. Love was a slow process, a gradual learning, appreciation, understanding. An attunement of the senses.

Yet what they'd just shared was more than lust. That much she knew. Lust didn't leave you caught up with introspective thought, wishing for something beyond reach, or cause you to wonder if what had just happened could irreparably change your life. Or if, she decided a trifle wildly, there would be any choice.

There was no magic wand she could wave to remove the past few hours. Tomorrow would be dealt with when it arrived. Now all she wanted to do, all she had the energy for, was sleep.

She was unaware of Nikos carefully shifting her to lay at his side, or that she instinctively curled into the curve of his body as he settled the bed-covering over her sleeping form.

*   *   *

Michelle felt something soft drift across her arm, and she burrowed her head more deeply into the pillow. It was early, her alarm hadn't sounded, and she was tired.

Minutes later there it was again, whispering along the curve of her waist. It had to be an early morning breeze teasing the sheet, and she kicked the tangle of soft percale, freeing it from her body.

This time there was no mistaking the brush of skin on skin, and her eyes swept open to see Nikos propped up on one elbow, watching her. His expression was slumberous and deceptively indolent, and he looked as sexy as hell with stubble darkening his jaw.

She'd experienced the entire gamut of emotions in his arms. Physical, emotional, spiritual had combined to make their coupling as good as she imagined it could possibly get.

Even thinking about what they'd shared brought a surge of heat flooding her body, and her eyes widened as he stroked gentle fingers over her breast. The sensitive peak hardened beneath his touch, and she drew in her breath as he rolled it gently between thumb and forefinger. Answering sensation flowered deep within, instantly so she ached with need, and her breathing hitched as he leaned forward and began teasing her breast with his lips.

His hand trailed low, conducting a seeking path with unerring accuracy, and within seconds she scaled the heights, begging as he held her there, then she tipped over the brink in a sensual free fall that left her breathing ragged, her voice an indistinguishable groan as she whispered his name.

He slid into her in one deep movement, nestled momentarily, then slowly withdrew, only to repeat the controlled thrust again and again. There was little of the hard passion of the night, just long and sweet and slow as she became consumed by a deep pulsing flame, intensely exquisite as it swirled and shimmered through her body like a treacherous heat haze.

She decided dreamily that it was a wonderful way to start the day.

'You have the most beautiful smile.'

'Mmm?'

His husky laughter curled round her nerve-ends and tugged just a little too much for comfort, activating a renewed spiral of sensation infinitely dangerous to an equilibrium already off balance.

Assertiveness was the key, she determined as she reached out and ran an idle forefinger down the slope of his nose. And humour.

'Time to begin all those mundane things like shower, breakfast, and don the business suit.' She traced the groove creasing his upper lip, then pressed down on the fullness beneath it, only to have him take her fingertip between his teeth. 'Ouch, that hurt.'

'It was meant to,' Nikos chided solemnly, although his eyes were darkly alight with amusement. 'We have an hour.'

Her heart lurched. 'I dislike being rushed.'

'I don't think you'll object.'

'Personal grooming,' Michelle said helplessly as he slid out of bed. 'A leisurely breakfast,' she intimated as he scooped her into his arms. 'And two cups of coffee. Where are you taking me?'

'The shower.' He reached the en suite bathroom in a few long strides. 'You can have that second coffee at the Gallery.'

With economy of movement he turned on the water dial, adjusted it, then stepped into the large glassed cubicle.

Nikos picked up the huge sponge, poured perfumed liquid soap onto it, then became intent on smoothing the sponge over every inch of her body.

It was an erotic experience, as he meant it to be, and she balled her hand into a fist and playfully struck his shoulder.

'Is that a complaint?'

The thought of sharing this kind of morning experience on a regular basis made her mouth go dry.

'Yes. I think I'm going to miss breakfast.'

His eyes were impossibly dark with lambent emotion as he lowered his head down to hers. 'Then I guess tomorrow we'll just have to make an earlier start, hmm?'

She didn't answer. She couldn't. The words were locked in her throat as his mouth took possession of her own.

She became oblivious to the warm spray of water, for there was only the hard strength of his body. Strong muscle and sinew that bound her close, so impossibly close that all she had to do was wind her arms up around his neck and hang on as he parted her thighs.

His arousal was a potent force he withheld in a bid to heighten her desire, and she was almost crazy with need when he finally surged into her. She cried out as sensation washed through her body, taking her higher than she'd thought it was possible to climb.

His mouth ravaged hers as he reached the physical peak with her, and she exulted in the primitive shudder that shook his large frame as they clung to each other in mutual climactic rapture and its aftermath.

Michelle missed breakfast entirely. There wasn't even time to do more than take a few hurried sips of the coffee Nikos brewed while she put the finishing touches to her make-up.

'I'll book the restaurant,' Nikos intimated as she collected her shoulder bag and turned towards the door. 'We're dining with Emilio and Saska, remember?' he prompted as she swivelled to face him, 'By the way,' he gently teased, 'Cute butterfly tattoo.'

It was small, and positioned low on the soft curve of her right buttock.

His smile was slow, musing. 'A moment of madness, flouting of parental authority, or what?'

'A dare. Paris.' A mischievous gleam lit her eyes. 'It was the tattoo or a navel ring.'

The phone rang, and for a moment the humour drained away. If it was Jeremy— She crossed the room and picked up the receiver.

'Michelle? Everything OK?'

Relief poured through her. 'Emilio. Yes. I'm just leaving now.' She cut the connection, and looked at Nikos. 'Just—lock up when you leave.'

'I'll contact my lawyer and set the paperwork in motion for a restraining order, then ring you.'

She was already crossing the lounge. 'Thanks.'

A chill slithered down her spine as she rode the lift down to the underground car park. The thought of Jeremy and just how close she'd come to assault was the reason why Nikos had stayed overnight in her apartment.

Not part of the agenda had been their shared intimacy. Who had initiated it?

Dear heaven, did it matter?

Michelle discovered that it did, very much, for it made a farce of their charade, and provided an unexpected twist in that they no longer needed to pretend.

A paradox really, for the lines determining their supposed relationship had shifted. For the better, if one believed in a transitory affair. Sadly, she didn't. What had begun as a mutual arrangement, now took on a different context. Jeremy was an unknown quantity. And there was Saska.

How long would it take to effect a resolution? A week? Two? Then what? Would Nikos extricate himself, move base to wherever in the world he chose, and never seek to contact her again?

That surely was part of the master plan. It had to be.

Wasn't that what she'd wanted?

The Gallery was just up front, and she parked the car, locked it, then ran up the short flight of steps to the main door.

Work, she decided, was a panacea for many things. All she had to do was keep herself busy, her mind occupied, and deal with each day as it occurred.

A hollow bubble of laughter rose and died in her throat. In theory, the analogy was fine. The problem was reality.

CHAPTER EIGHT

THE mobile phone rang as Michelle eased the car onto the road, and she assured her mother she was fine, she'd slept well; and no, she hadn't forgotten the charity function at a city hotel scheduled for Thursday evening.

'Nikos can partner you, darling. You'll sit at our table, of course.'

Michelle parked outside the Gallery, and cut the connection as she reached the main entrance.

It proved to be a hectic morning. A shipment due to be unloaded from a dockside container in Sydney was caught up in a strike, and numerous phone calls were necessary to reschedule and put a contingency plan in place.

There was paperwork requiring attention, data to enter into the computer, and several

phone calls to make confirming collection
and delivery of items ordered on consign-
ment.

The phone pealed, and she automatically
reached for the receiver and intoned a professional greeting.

'Michelle. Nikos.'

His voice was deeper and slightly more accented over the phone, and the sound of it
evoked a pulsing warmth flooding her veins.

'I've arranged an appointment with my
lawyer at twelve-thirty.'

The restraining order. 'I'll reorganise my
lunch hour.'

'I'll meet you at the Gallery and take you
to Paul's office,' Nikos intimated, and she
sank back in her chair, swivelled it to take in
the view across the Nerang river.

'I don't think that's necessary.'

'Twelve-fifteen, Michelle.'

He hung up before she had the opportunity
to argue.

'Problems?'

Michelle swung back to face Emilio, who had walked into the office during the conversation. 'Nothing I can't handle.' It was said more to convince herself than Emilio. Somehow she didn't think any woman could manipulate Nikos. Unless he permitted it.

'You left early last night.'

It was better she went with the fictional excuse. 'I had a headache.'

He placed both hands on the desk and leaned forward. 'This is Emilio, remember?'

She kept her gaze steady as he raked her pale features, then settled on the pulse at the base of her throat.

'So, do we play guessing games, or are you going to tell me?'

'OK.' She used facetiousness and shock value as a form of defence. 'Nikos took me home, and we made wild passionate love all night.'

His eyes lit with amusement, and something else she was unable to define. *'Brava,'* he said gently. 'I approve. Of the loving, and the Greek.' He straightened away from the desk. 'Jeremy was the catalyst, am I right? For someone who knew what to look for last night, it wasn't difficult to put two and two together. Your absence, Jeremy, then Nikos.' His expression hardened fractionally. 'I'll wring his neck.'

'Jeremy, or the Greek?'

'Don't jest, *cara*. If there's a problem, I want to know about it.' He waited a beat. 'We're more than just business partners, we're friends.'

She spent a major part of her waking hours at the Gallery. Emilio deserved to be on the alert if Jeremy continued to prove a nuisance.

'Nikos insists I file a restraining order.'

Emilio's eyes sharpened. 'Give,' he uttered in succinct command.

'Last night was the third—' *Assault?* She settled for '—attack, in seventy-two hours.'

'Son of a bitch!' The words were uttered with such silky softness, it sent a shiver down her back. 'He won't get a foot inside the

Gallery. Your apartment is secure.' His expression became ruthlessly hard. 'Don't go anywhere alone. *Comprende?*'

'I just love it when you lapse into Italian,' Michelle teased at his protective stance.

'I'm serious.'

She tilted her head to one side, her eyes solemn. 'I'm a big girl. And capable of defending myself, remember?'

She was good, he visited the same *dojo* and had witnessed a few of her training sessions. However, expertise in formal surroundings was a different kettle of fish to the reality of an unexpected attack with brutal intent in a dark deserted street.

'Stand up,' he instructed quietly. 'Turn with your back to me.'

'Emilio—'

'Do it, *cara.*'

'This really is unnecessary,' she protested, and caught his faint smile.

'Indulge me.'

The electronic buzzer attached to the main door sounded, heralding entrance of a customer, and Emilio spared a quick glance in the overhead monitor.

'Nikos.'

It was twelve-fifteen already? She should go powder her nose and ensure her hair was OK.

'We'll continue this later.'

'What will you continue later?' Nikos drawled from the open doorway.

His tall frame almost filled the aperture, and Michelle was positive the room seemed to shrink in size. He looked the epitome of an urbane sophisticate attired in impeccably cut trousers, a dark blue shirt unbuttoned at the neck and a jacket hooked casually over one shoulder.

'A test against a real attack attempt, as opposed to an orchestrated practised manoeuvre,' Emilio enlightened, meeting Nikos' steady gaze with one of his own.

'Michelle has filled you in.' It was a statement, not a question.

'Yes.'

'I take it you have no objection if she has an extended lunch hour?'

'As long as it takes.'

'I'm moving her into my apartment.'

Michelle thrust the swivel chair forward, and glared from one man to the other. 'Now, just wait a damn minute.' She settled on Nikos. '*Excuse me.* You're doing *what?*'

'Moving you temporarily into my apartment,' he reiterated calmly.

Her eyes flashed emerald fire. 'The hell you are.'

'Then I'll move into yours. Either way, it makes little difference.'

'It makes plenty of difference!'

'Then choose.'

'Just who has granted you the God-given right to take over my life and order me around?' She was so furious, her body was almost rigid with anger.

'I did,' Nikos relayed with deceptive ease. 'Your apartment, or mine, *pedhaki mou?*'

'I am *not* "your little one"!'

Nikos' eyes flared. 'Yes, you are.'

Emilio watched the by-play with interest. Intriguing the sparks that flew between these two. He smiled, despite the gravity of the situation at hand. Unless he was very wrong, Michelle had met her match in the forceful Greek.

'I'd rather move home.'

Nikos shook his head. 'Due to your parents' social commitments, they're rarely in residence except for a few requisite hours each night, and they don't have live-in help.'

'While you,' she vented with deliberate emphasis, 'intend to stand guard over me every minute of the day?'

'And night,' he added equably, although his tone was deceptive. The eyes had it. Inflexible, compelling. Invincible.

'No.' She refused to be ordered about like a child.

'No?' His voice was pure silk.

'I'll book into a hotel.'

'Where, without independent security, Jeremy could access your room in a minute?'

'Don't you think,' she inclined carefully, 'you're getting just a bit carried with all this?'

'I have your parents' approval.'

'That's a low trick.'

'They're just as concerned about your safety as I am.'

She was angry, so angry at the way he was taking control. 'I don't doubt that. But I can take care of myself. I don't need a minder, or a baby-sitter!'

He wanted to take hold of her shoulders and shake her. Instead, he used words to create a similar effect.

'Jeremy has a history of previous violence. In this instance, it's been activated by his jealousy of me and what he sees as my involvement with you. Which makes me responsible to a degree.'

He looked at her carefully. 'What if I hadn't been there when he accosted you outside the Gallery Sunday night?' It gave him little pleasure to see her eyes dilate at his implication. 'Or last night?' he pursued relentlessly. 'Was anyone else aware Jeremy might use any opportunity to get you alone? Was there anyone who became alarmed when you didn't return within a reasonable time?'

He paused, then slid home the final barb. 'Have you considered what would have happened had I not come in search of you when I did?'

She opened her mouth to refute what he'd said, then closed it again.

'Jeremy has attacked you three times,' Emilio stated inexorably. 'You want to try for four?'

Nikos' eyes pierced hers, their depths dark and inflexible. 'Don't you think you're protesting too much... after last night?'

He was too skilled a tactician not to choose his weapons well, she perceived, and silently cursed him for his temerity.

'Aren't we late for an appointment?' she posed stiffly, and heard his drawled response.

'I'll ring Paul and let him know we've been delayed.'

'If it's all right with you,' Michelle declared with deliberate mockery, 'I'll just go powder my nose.'

Nikos Alessandros, she decided, had a lot to answer for. At this very moment her feelings were definitely ambivalent.

Damn, damn, *damn*. Why was she objecting? The man was a lover to die for. Why not just go with the flow, enjoy the perks, and live for the day?

Last night had been *heaven*. Was it such a sin to enjoy responsible sex?

Without commitment? And what happens when it ends, as it inevitably will? a small imp taunted. What then? Do you think you'll be able to walk away, heart-whole, smile, and thank him for the memory?

'Give me a break,' she pleaded with the inimical imp, snapped on the lid of her lipstick, then she reentered the office and shot Nikos a dark glance.

Which merely resulted in a raised eyebrow. 'Ready?'

'Take your time,' Emilio bade as Michelle preceded Nikos out onto the mezzanine balcony.

They traversed the short flight of stairs down to the main Gallery.

'Do what you need to do, and if you don't make it back by five, I'll see you at the restaurant at six.'

'I'll be back midafternoon,' she declared firmly, as she leant forward and brushed Emilio's cheek.

Nikos unlocked the BMW and she slid into the passenger seat, watched as he crossed round to slip in behind the wheel, then she sat in silence as he eased the large car into the flow of traffic heading towards the main highway.

'You're very quiet.'

'I'm saving it all for later,' she assured, and heard his husky laughter. 'If you weren't driving, I'd *hit* you,' she said fiercely.

Southport was merely a few kilometres distant, and within five minutes Nikos drove into a client car park adjacent a modern glassed building.

Nikos' lawyer led her through a series of questions as he compiled a detailed draft statement, informed what a restraining order entailed, perused a sheaf of faxed reports Nikos provided him with, then he advised her as to her personal safety, and requested she call into the office at four that afternoon to sign the statement.

It was one-thirty when they emerged from the building, and within minutes Nikos headed the car towards Main Beach.

'Where are you going?' Michelle queried sharply when he turned towards the Sheraton hotel and its adjacent marina shopping complex.

'Taking you to lunch.'

'I'm not hungry.'

'The seafood buffet should tempt your appetite.'

'Nikos—'

'I've never known a woman who argues the way you do,' he drawled with amusement.

'You,' she stated heatedly. 'Are the most domineering man I've ever met!'

He eased the BMW into an empty parking space and killed the engine. Then he released his seat belt and leaned towards her.

His mouth settled on hers, hard, as he shaped her jaw to his, and he employed a sensual ravishment that tore her anger to shreds and left her breathless and trembling.

She was incapable of uttering a word, and he brushed a gentle finger over her lower lip.

'You talk too much.' He reached for the clip of her seat belt, released it, then he slid out from behind the wheel and led her towards the restaurant.

It was peaceful to sit overlooking the huge pool with its lagoon bar, and the buffet offered a superb selection which proved too tempting for Michelle to resist.

'Feel better?' Nikos queried when she declined dessert and settled for coffee.

'Yes,' she answered simply.

'We need to discuss whose apartment we share.'

'I don't think—'

'Yours or mine?'

'Are you always this dictatorial?'

'It's an integral part of my personality.' The waiter presented the bill, and Nikos signed the credit slip, added a tip, then he drained the last of his coffee. 'Shall we leave?'

Within minutes Nikos turned the car into the street housing both their apartment buildings, and she opened her mouth to protest when he swept down into the car park beneath his building.

'Come up with me while I collect some clothes.'

She turned towards him. 'I don't like people making decisions for me.'

His expression assumed an inflexibility, accenting the vertical grooves down each cheek, and his mouth settled into a firm line. 'Get used to it, *pedhi mou.*'

Michelle rode the lift with him to the uppermost floor. 'We're going to have to draw a few ground rules,' she insisted as she entered his penthouse apartment.

It was beautiful, marble tiled floors, Oriental rugs, imported furniture and exquisite furnishings. Interior decorating at its finest.

'Make yourself comfortable,' Nikos bade. 'I won't be long.'

There were a few framed photographs positioned on a long mahogany table, and she crossed to examine them. Family, she perceived, noting an elderly couple pictured in one, while the others were presumably siblings with a number of young children.

She knew so little about him, his background. Why, when his family obviously resided in Europe, he chose to spend part of his time in Australia.

Which inevitably led to how long he intended to stay on this particular occasion. Weeks, or a month or two? With business interests on several different continents, he wouldn't remain in one place for very long at a time.

Nikos returned to the lounge with a garment bag hooked over one shoulder, and a hold-all in his hand.

'Two sisters,' he revealed, anticipating her question. 'Both married. One lives in Athens, the other in London. My parents reside on Santorini.'

'While you wander the world.' She could imagine the high-powered existence he led. International flights, board meetings, wheeling and dealing.

'I have houses in several countries.'

'And a woman in each city?'

'I have many women friends,' he said with dry mockery.

Now why did that suddenly make her feel bereft? Did she really think *she* was different? Special? Get real, an inner voice mercilessly taunted. You're simply a momentary diversion.

With determined effort she spared her watch a glance and turned towards the door. 'Shall we leave?' She needed some space and time away from him. 'You can drop me off at the Gallery. I'll give you a key to my apartment.'

Minutes later he drew the car to a halt outside the Gallery. 'I'll pick you up at five.'

She was about to argue, but one look at his implacable expression was sufficient to change her mind, and she refrained from saying a word as she handed him her keys, then she slid out, closed the door, and trod the bricked path to the Gallery's main entrance without so much as a backward glance.

If Emilio was surprised to see her, he didn't say so, and she went straight through to the office and booted up the computer.

With determined resolve she set her mind on work, and refused to give Nikos Alessandros a second thought.

Until he appeared with Emilio in the doorway a few minutes after five.

'Time to close down for the day, *cara.*'

Michelle saved the data, closed the programme and shut down the machine. Without a word she collected her bag and preceded Nikos out to the car.

It was a bright summer's evening, the sun was still warm, and she could easily have walked. She wasn't sure whether it bothered her more that her freedom of choice had been endangered, or that Nikos had nominated himself as her protector.

Or perhaps she was more shaken at the thought of sharing her apartment with him.

Last night... Hell, she didn't even want to think about last night!

Nikos parked in the bay next to hers, and they rode the lift to the fifteenth floor in silence.

Nikos unlocked her apartment, and she swept in ahead of him.

'Fix yourself a drink if you want one,' Michelle suggested politely as she tossed her bag down onto the coffee table. 'I'm going to shower and change.'

She entered her bedroom and went straight to the walk-in wardrobe. If he'd *dared* invade her space by hanging his clothes here...

He hadn't, and she told herself she was glad as she entered the shower.

Half an hour later she caught up an evening purse and paused in front of the cheval mirror to briefly examine her appearance.

The emerald-coloured evening pantsuit complemented her slim frame and highlighted her eyes. Minimum jewellery and an upswept hairstyle presented an essential sophisticated image, given that Saska would undoubtedly appear at her stunning best.

Michelle took a deep breath, released it, then joined Nikos in the lounge.

His appraisal was swift, encompassing, and caused a shivery sensation to scud across the surface of her skin.

She offered him a brilliant smile. 'Do you think Saska will be impressed?'

He didn't offer a word as he crossed the short distance to her side, and her eyes widened as he cradled her face, then settled his mouth on hers in passionate possession.

When he lifted his head she wasn't capable of saying so much as a word.

'Better,' he drawled. He touched the pad of one finger to her lips. 'Lipstick repair.' The edge of his mouth curved. 'Although personally, I prefer the natural look.'

'Don't overdo the play-acting,' she managed evenly. 'I doubt Saska will be fooled.'

It was just after six when they reached the nominated restaurant, and within minutes

Emilio and Saska joined them in the lounge bar.

As Michelle predicted, Saska could have stepped from one of the fashion pages of *Vogue*. In classic black, the style was deceptively demure...a total contradiction when Saska removed the fitted bolero top to reveal the dress was virtually strapless, with a thin shoestring strap over each shoulder.

'It's a little warm in here, don't you think?'

Oh my. Were those generous curves for real? They just begged to be shaped and caressed by a man's hand.

She caught Emilio's eye, saw the faint glimmer of amusement apparent, and prepared to shift gears into 'compete' mode.

This was, Michelle accorded silently, going to be quite an evening!

'Michelle,' Saska almost purred. 'One hopes you no longer suffer from your headache?'

The faint emphasis gave the malady quite a different interpretation. 'Nikos took good care of me.'

How was that for an understatement? If Saska were to guess the manner in which he'd cared for her, the sparks would surely fly!

It was fortuitous the maître d' chose that moment to indicate their table was ready, and within minutes the wine steward appeared to take their order.

CHAPTER NINE

'CHAMPAGNE?' Saska suggested. 'We should drink to our continuing friendship.'

'Yes,' Michelle agreed with a winsome smile. 'Why don't we do that?'

'Nikos and I go back a long way.'

'So he told me.'

Saska's eyebrow arched. 'I imagine you know I was married to his best friend?'

'You must miss him very much,' she said gently. Saska deserved some compassion. It would be devastating to be widowed at any age, but for someone so young, the loss must be terrible.

Eyes dark and faintly cloudy regarded Michelle with contrived steadiness. 'Dreadfully. But life moves on, and so must I.'

With Nikos, Michelle deduced. She could hardly blame Saska for pursuing the possibility. Nikos was a man among men, irrespective of his wealth, status and social position. As a lover... Just the thought of what she'd shared with him was enough to melt her bones.

Nikos ordered a bottle of Dom Pérignon, and together they perused the menu, their choices varied as they deliberated over a starter, main and dessert.

The waiter presented the champagne with a flourish, eased off the cork, then part-filled each flute before setting the bottle in the ice bucket and retreating.

'To old friends,' Saska said gently, touching the rim of her flute to that of Nikos'.

His answering smile was equally gentle, then he silently saluted Emilio and turned to Michelle.

'To us.'

His eyes were dark, and so incredibly sensual, she had to consciously prevent her eyes dilating with shock.

Her mouth shook slightly as he caught her hand and linked her fingers with his.

He'd missed his vocation as an actor. If she hadn't known better, she could almost believe he meant the light touch on her arm, the slight brush of his fingers against her cheek. The warmth of his smile, the way his eyes gleamed with latent emotion.

Together, they decided on a selection from each course, gave their order, then discussed a range of topics from art to travel as they sipped champagne.

Emilio added authenticity to Nikos and Michelle's 'romance' with anecdotes from his years as an art student in France.

'Remember, *cara?* That little café on the Left Bank, where the waiter plied you with coffee and pledged his undying love?'

Saska looked from one to the other, her fork poised as she posed a question. 'You studied together and shared accommodation?'

Michelle wrinkled her nose, then laughed, a faint husky sound that was unintentionally sexy. 'Yes, with four other students. Communal kitchen, bathroom. Tiny rooms. It was little more than a garret.'

'But you adored it,' Emilio endorsed. 'Too much coffee, too little food, and too much discussion on how to change the world.'

'You lived in a garret?' Saska queried in disbelief. 'With little money? Didn't your parents help you?'

'Of course. Except I didn't want a nice apartment in the right quarter, with smoked salmon and caviar in the fridge.'

'She gave all that up for the baguettes, sardines, and cheese.'

'And wine,' Michelle added with an impish smile. 'It was fun.'

'Pretending to be poor?'

'Dispensing with the trappings of the rich,' she corrected with quiet sincerity. 'Had I not done that, my time in Paris would have been very different.'

'Yet you managed to meet Nikos.' Saska gave a faint disbelieving laugh. 'I cannot imagine him slumming it.'

'We met at the home of mutual friends,' Nikos drawled, embellishing the original fabrication.

'It was one of those rare occasions when we ventured into the sophisticated arena of the rich Parisians,' Emilio revealed with droll cynicism.

'So you were at the party, too?'

'As Michelle's bodyguard,' he declared solemnly. 'She rarely left home without me. And no,' he added quietly at Saska's deliberately raised eyebrows. 'We were never more than just very good friends.'

'And now you're business partners.'

Emilio inclined his head in mocking acquiescence. 'Our friendship is based on trust. What better foundation to establish a business?'

'How—quaint,' Saska acknowledged. 'Pretending to be impoverished students, then returning home to open a Gallery.'

You don't get it, do you? Michelle queried silently. We needed the struggle, the very essence that combines naked ambition with the perspicacity to survive and succeed. A nebulous element that shows in the art as something more than talent. We wanted to be able to recognise that flair through personal experience, not as judgmental eclectics.

It was perhaps as well the waiter delivered the starter. Although she wasn't so sure as Nikos played the part of attentive lover by tempting her with a morsel of food from his plate.

It was relatively easy to take up his challenge by spearing a succulent prawn from its bed of lettuce and offering it to him from the edge of her fork. She even managed to adopt the role of temptress with a melting smile, which brought an answering gleam and a flash of white teeth as he took a bite of the fleshy seafood.

Michelle daren't glance in Emilio's direction, for if he acknowledged her performance with a surreptitious wink she would be in danger of subsiding into laughter, and that would totally destroy the illusion.

Saska was not about to be outdone. Although her attempts to gain Nikos' attention were infinitely more subtle with the light touch of her hand on his arm, the few 're-member' anecdotes that served to endorse a long friendship.

Michelle had to concede it was a fun evening, for she enjoyed the nuances, the interplay, and the elusive rivalry, albeit that on her part it was contrived.

Or was it? There was nothing false about her reaction to Nikos' touch. Or the warmth that radiated through her body when he smiled. The brush of his lips caused a spiral of sensation encompassing every nerve cell.

It provided a vivid reminder of the exquisite orgasmic experience they'd shared, and the need to recapture it again.

Which would be the height of foolishness. Sexual gratification was no substitute for lovemaking. It was something she'd vowed to uphold. Selective sex with someone she cared for, and who she believed cared for her. It didn't sit well that last night she'd broken her own rule.

They chose to decline dessert in favour of the cheeseboard, and lingered over excellent coffee.

Michelle was surprised to see it was after eleven when they parted outside the restaurant, and she offered her cheek for Emilio's kiss.

'*Brava,* darling,' he murmured close to her ear, then offered, 'Your performance was incredible. See you in the morning.'

Saska followed suit by pressing her lips to Nikos' cheek, then lightly, briefly on his mouth. 'We must do this again soon.'

Nikos' smile held warmth. 'We'll look forward to it.' He caught Michelle's hand and threaded her fingers through his own, then brought it to his lips. 'Won't, we?'

Oh my, he was good. She offered him a melting smile. 'Of course. Thursday evening there's a charity ball being held at the Marriott. *Maman* is on the committee. I can arrange a ticket if Saska would like to join us.'

Saska didn't hesitate. 'I'd love to.'

Nikos waited until they were seated in the car before venturing with silky amusement, 'Do you delight in setting the cat among the pigeons?'

Michelle turned towards him and offered a stunning smile. 'Why, *darling, Maman* will be gratified at the sale of another ticket, and Saska will enjoy the evening.'

'And you, *pedhaki mou,*' he drawled. 'What will you enjoy?'

'Watching you,' she responded sweetly.

'Playing the part? Isn't that what we all do on occasion? In business, socially?'

'You do it exceptionally well.'

'Let me return the compliment.'

'In the interest of establishing our pseudo relationship, the evening was a success.'

He didn't answer as he negotiated an intersection, and she lapsed into a silence that stretched the several minutes it took to reach her apartment building.

'There's no need for you to stay,' Michelle declared firmly as he rode the lift with her to the fifteenth floor.

'We've already settled this issue.'

'Last night was different.' The lift came to a halt and she retrieved her key in readiness.

'No.'

She crossed the carpeted lobby to her apartment and unlocked the door.

'What do you mean—*no?*'

'Your apartment or mine,' Nikos reiterated hardily. 'It's irrelevant. But we share.'

'I doubt Jeremy will attempt to enter the building, and even if he did, he'd never get past my front door.'

He thrust a hand into each trouser pocket, and looked at her with open cynicism. 'You don't think he's sufficiently devious to disguise himself as a delivery messenger?' He continued before she had a chance to answer. 'Or utilise some plausible ploy to get past reception?'

A week ago none of these possibilities would have entered her head. Now, she had good reason to pause for thought. And she didn't like any of the answers.

'You're not prepared to give in, are you?' she queried wearily.

'No.'

She didn't say a further word, and simply turned and walked through to the kitchen. She needed a drink. Hot sweet tea to take the edge off the champagne and an excellent meal.

Michelle filled the electric kettle and switched it on, then she extracted a cup, tea-bag, sugar and milk, and stood waiting for the water to boil.

She was conscious of Nikos' presence, and all too aware of him silently watching her actions as she poured hot water into the cup, sweetened it and added milk.

If he stayed there much longer, she'd be tempted to throw something at him.

She discarded the spoon into the sink, and looked at him. Then wished she hadn't.

Eyes that were dark and frighteningly still held her own captive, and she felt like an animal caught in a trap.

Everything faded into the background, and there was only a mesmeric quality apparent as he closed the distance between them.

'Fight me, argue with me,' Nikos berated silkily. 'But don't turn your back and walk away.' He lifted a hand and caught hold of her chin between thumb and forefinger, then tilted it. 'Ever.'

It was impossible to escape that deep assessing gaze, and her own anger lent an edge of defiance.

'Don't say a word,' he warned with deceptive mildness, as she opened her mouth to give vent to his actions.

'Why?'

His mouth angled over hers, then took possession in a kiss which tore the breath from her throat as he plundered at will.

Then the pressure eased, and she almost cried out as he began an evocative tasting with such sensual mastery it was almost all she could do not to respond.

A flame deep within ignited and flared into vibrant life, until her whole body was consumed with it, and she wound her arms up around his neck, leaned into him, and simply went with whatever he dictated.

It was a long time before he gradually broke contact, and she could only look at him in stunned silence as he lightly traced the swollen contours of her mouth.

'There's no one here to observe the pretense,' Michelle said shakily, and his smile held musing warmth.

'Who says it's a pretense?'

His hand brushed across her collarbone, back and forth in a hypnotic movement, and she bit back a gasp as he settled his lips at the base of her throat.

'Let's not do this,' she pleaded fruitlessly, and felt his mouth part in a soundless smile.

'Frightened?'

'Scared witless,' she admitted.

He savoured the sweet valley between her breasts, then slowly nibbled his way back to her lips. 'Don't be.'

She had to stop him now, or she'd never find the willpower to break away.

'Last night was a mistake,' she said desperately, and almost died at the force of his arousal.

'Something which felt so good could never be a mistake.'

Michelle made a last-ditch effort. 'Foolish, then,' she amended.

'What makes you say that?'

Self-preservation and remorse reared its head. 'I don't do this sort of thing,' she assured, then attempted to clarify. 'We haven't even known each other a week.'

His eyes held hers, and there was wry humour, sensuality, and something else she couldn't define. 'A lifetime,' he mocked lightly.

'It has to mean something,' she protested.

'And this doesn't?'

'No—yes. Oh hell. I don't know.' She was supremely conscious of the sensual warmth stealing through her veins, heating her body until her bones seemed to liquify and dissolve beneath the flood of sensation.

She felt bare, exposed, and frighteningly vulnerable, and she needed to explain why. 'I like to plan things, have a reason for everything. Not dive off the deep end with—'

'Someone you've known less than a week?'

'Yes!' She was out of her depth, and flailing. 'Where can this—this farce, possibly lead? In a few weeks it'll all be over. Then what?'

Nikos brushed gentle fingers down her cheek and let them rest at the edge of her mouth.

'Why not wait and see?'

Because I don't want to be hurt, she cried silently. Too late, a tiny gremlin taunted. You're already in this up to your neck, and in a one-sided love, pain is part of the deal.

Love? She didn't love him. Lust, maybe. Definitely lust, she amended as he hoisted her high up against him and walked towards the bedroom.

Michelle wound her legs around his waist and held on, exulting in the feel of him, the broad expanse of his chest, the tight waist, the strength of his arms.

In the bedroom he switched on the lamp, then let her slide down to her feet.

For a moment she just looked at him, then he lowered his head and took her mouth, gently this time, employing such acute sensitivity she felt she might cry.

Together, they slowly divested their clothes, pausing every now and again to brush a tantalising path over bare flesh in a teasing discovery.

She adored the texture of his skin, the hard ridges of muscle and sinew, the clean faint musky aroma. There was the faint tightening of muscle, the soft intake of breath as she caressed him, and she groaned out loud when he wreaked havoc with one sensitive peak, then the other as he suckled at each breast.

There were no questions asked, no answers given, as they embarked on a sensual feast that was alternately gentle and slow, then so hard and fast sweat beaded their skin and their breath became tortured and ragged.

It was a long night, with little sleep, only the mutual sharing of something infinitely special. Wholly sexual, blissfully sensual, and to Michelle, incredibly unique.

On the edge of exhaustion she wondered if it all wasn't a figment of her fervent imagination. Except there was a hard male body to which she clung, and something terribly *real* to the scent and feel of him.

'Orange juice, shower, breakfast, work,' a husky male voice tormented. 'Rise and shine, *pedhi mou*. You have forty minutes.'

Michelle lifted a hand, then let it fall back onto the bed. 'It's the middle of the night.'

'Eight-fifteen on a bright and warm Wednesday morning,' Nikos assured, and pulled the sheet from her supine form.

He could, he thought regretfully, get very interested in the slender lines of her back. The twin slopes of her bottom were firm mounds his hands itched to shape. And as for that daring little butterfly tattoo... It just begged to be kissed, tasted, and savoured. Like the cute dimple on each side of her lower spine.

'Five seconds,' he warned musingly. 'Or I'll join you, and you won't surface until midday.'

That had the desired effect, for she rolled onto her back and opened her eyes. 'Five?'

'Three, and counting,' Nikos assured, laughing softly as she swung her feet to the floor.

'Orange juice.' He handed her the glass and watched her drain half the contents before handing it back to him.

'Shower,' Michelle said obediently, and searched for her wrap.

'Nice view,' he complimented gently, and glimpsed the tinge of pink colour her cheeks.

'You're dressed,' she observed as she pushed a tumbled swathe of hair behind one ear.

'Showered, shaved, and I've just cooked breakfast.'

'A gem among men.' She found the wrap and shrugged her arms into it. 'I hope you've made coffee?'

'It's percolating.'

'Are you usually so energetic at this hour of the morning?' She caught his gleaming smile, and her mouth formed a wry grimace. 'Don't answer that.'

Michelle crossed to the en suite, and adjusted the water dial in the shower to hot. Afterwards she'd turn it to cold in the hope it would encourage her blood to circulate more quickly and force her into bright-eyed wakefulness.

A fifty per cent improvement was better than none, she perceived half an hour later as she sipped ruinously strong coffee and sliced banana onto cereal.

By the time she finished both, she felt almost human.

Five minutes remained to take the lift down, slip into her car and drive the short distance to the Gallery.

'I have meetings scheduled for most of the day,' Nikos informed as they took the lift together. 'I should be back about six. If there's any delay, I'll phone you.'

'Oh hell,' Michelle said inelegantly as they crossed to where their cars were parked.

'Problems?'

'A flat tyre.' Disbelief coloured her voice, and Nikos swore softly beneath his breath.

'I'll drop you off at the Gallery. Give me your car keys, and I'll arrange to have someone fix it.'

Closer examination revealed the tyre had been very neatly slashed.

'You don't think—'

'This is Jeremy's handiwork?' He was certain of it. 'Possibly.' Just as he was sure there would be no evidence.

He unlocked the BMW and Michelle slid into the passenger seat. Within seconds he fired the engine and eased the large car up the ramp and out onto the road.

Two blocks down he pulled into the kerb, let the engine idle, and reached across to unlatch her door. 'I'll ring you through the day.' He kissed her, hard, briefly, then straightened as she released the seat belt and stepped out from the car.

It was a hectic morning as Michelle caught up on a batch of invoices, liaised with the framing firm, and made countless phone calls.

Lunch was something she ate at her desk, and it came as something of a shock when Nikos rang at three-thirty.

'I've had your car delivered to the Gallery. Don't forget your four o'clock appointment with the lawyer. I'll collect you in fifteen minutes.'

Oh hell, she hadn't forgotten, she simply hadn't expected the time to come around so fast. 'Thanks.'

There was a sense of satisfaction in attaching her signature to the legal statement, and a degree of relief the matter was now in official hands.

It was almost five when Nikos drew the BMW to a halt outside the Gallery, and it was a simple matter to slip behind the wheel of her Porsche and followed him the few blocks to her apartment.

The message light was blinking on her answering machine, and she activated the button and listened to the recorded message.

''Eloise, Michelle. You haven't called. So this is a reminder. Don't forget Philippe's party tonight. Six-thirty.''

'Philippe?' Nikos queried.

'My godson,' she explained. 'He's three years old, and tonight is his day-care Christmas party.' She lifted a hand and pushed a stray lock of hair behind one ear. 'I can't believe I didn't remember.' She checked her watch. 'I'll have to shower, change and leave.'

'I'll come with you.'

Michelle cast him a wry glance. 'To a children's party?'

'To a children's party,' he repeated mockingly.

It was fun. Parents, family, gathered in front of a large open-air stage at the day-care centre, young children dressed in costume as the teachers led them through their practised paces. Taped music, and childish voices singing out of tune and synch. Smiles and laughter when some of the children forgot they were supposed to act and waved to their parents.

Michelle stood among the crowd, with Nikos positioned behind her, secure within the light circle of his arms.

Afterwards she searched for and found Eloise and her husband, and spent time with Philippe, who displayed his delight at her being there, as well as curiosity for the man at her side. She whispered in his ear in French, and made him giggle.

'I am a bon tot,' Philippe repeated in English to his parents. 'Tante Michelle says so.'

It was almost nine when the pageant concluded, and after bidding Philippe an affectionate goodnight she walked with Nikos to the car.

Minutes later she leaned back against the headrest and closed her eyes. It had been an eventful day, following on from a very eventful night.

When they stepped inside her apartment Nikos took one look at her pale features, the dark shadows beneath her eyes, and gently pushed her in the direction of her bedroom.

'Go to bed, *pedhaki mou.*'

She needed no second bidding, and within minutes she'd divested her clothes, cleansed her face of make-up and was laying supine beneath the bedcovers.

Sleep came almost instantly, and she woke in the morning, alone. Except the pillow beside hers held an indentation, and there was the soft musky aroma of male cologne as a vivid reminder that Nikos had shared her bed.

Michelle took a hurried shower, then she dressed ready for work and emerged into the kitchen to discover Nikos dressed and speaking into his mobile phone in a language she could only surmise as being his own.

One glance at the countertop was sufficient to determine he'd already eaten, and she finished a small plate of cereal with fruit before he'd completed his conversation.

'Good morning.' He crossed to her side, brushed her lips with his own, then he picked up a cup and drained his coffee. 'Almost ready? I'll drop you at the Gallery.'

CHAPTER TEN

IT HADN'T been the best of days, Michelle reflected as she entered her apartment just after five. Whatever could have gone wrong, had.

Nikos had called to say he'd be late, and while she told herself she was pleased to have the apartment to herself for more than an hour, that wasn't strictly true.

She craved the warmth of his arms, the feel of his mouth on hers, the heat that pulsed through her veins at the mere thought of him.

The light on her answering machine blinked, and she ran the message tape, only to hear three hang-ups, which she considered mildly disturbing, given that her mobile number was recorded for contact.

Jeremy? Would he revert to nuisance hang-up calls?

A shower would do much to ease the tension, and ten minutes later she donned denim cut-offs, a fitted rib-knit top, left her hair loose, and applied minimum make-up. It was way too early to begin dressing for the charity ball, and she didn't fancy floating around the apartment for more than an hour in a wrap.

The intercom buzzed, and she crossed to activate it.

There was silence for a few seconds. 'Having fun with your live-in lover, Michelle?'

A sickening feeling twisted her stomach at the sound of Jeremy's voice, and she released the intercom, only to hear it buzz again almost immediately. She hugged her arms together, hesitated, then picked up the receiver.

Her fingers clenched, and her voice assumed an unaccustomed hardness. 'Don't be a fool, Jeremy.'

'Wisdom isn't my forte.'

'What do you hope to achieve by harassing me?'

'Haven't you worked it out yet? I find it a challenge to skate close to the law and remain unscathed.'

She hung up on him, and almost didn't answer the phone when it rang twenty minutes later.

'Michelle? We have a delivery of flowers for you at reception.'

Michelle's lips curved into a smile. 'I'll be right down.' She caught up her key and went out to summon the lift.

A beautiful bouquet of carnations in delicate pastels encased in clear cellophane greeted her, and she reached for the attached envelope.

A single word was slashed in black, and showed starkly against the white embossed card. *Bitch.*

She didn't need to question who'd sent them.

'Will you dump these for me?'

'Excuse me?'

'Dump them,' Michelle repeated firmly.

'But they're beautiful,' the receptionist declared with shocked surprise.

'Unfortunately the intention behind them isn't.'

A fleeting movement on the bricked apron beyond the automatic glass entrance doors caught her eye, and she recognised Jeremy execute an elaborate bow before he moved quickly out of sight.

It was a deliberate taunt. A reminder that he was choosing to play a dangerous game by his own rules.

'It seems a shame to waste them.'

Michelle merely shrugged her shoulders and headed towards the double bank of lifts.

She had an hour in which to change, apply make-up and do something with her hair.

The thought of attending a pre-Christmas ball to aid a prominent charity held little appeal. Women spent days preparing for this particular annual event. Chantelle, she knew, would have gone from the masseuse to the beautician, had her nails lacquered, then spent hours with the hairdresser.

Ten minutes later she'd stripped down to briefs, added a silky wrap, then she crossed to the vanity to begin applying make-up.

It was there that Nikos found her, and he wondered at the faint shadows beneath her eyes, the slightly too bright smile.

'Bad day?' He felt his loins tighten as she leaned close to the mirror.

'So-so,' Michelle answered cautiously.

'Are you wearing anything beneath that wrap?' he queried conversationally.

She glimpsed the purposeful gleam apparent in those dark eyes, and shook her head in silent mockery. 'There's not enough time.'

His smile tugged at her heart and did strange things to the nerves in her stomach. 'We could always arrive late.'

'No,' she declared. 'We couldn't.'

He moved to stand behind her, and her eyes dilated at their mirrored image. One so tall and dark-haired, while the top of her blond head barely reached his shoulder.

His hands slid round her waist, released the belted tie, then moved to cup each breast.

Liquid warmth spilled through her veins, heating her body as desire, raw and primitive, activated each nerve cell.

Michelle watched with almost detached fascination as her skin quivered beneath the sweet sorcery of his touch, and she felt her breath catch as one hand splayed low over her abdomen, seeking, teasing the soft curling hair at the apex of her thighs.

The lacy bikini briefs were soon dispensed with, and when she would have turned into his arms he held her still, then he lowered his mouth to the curve of her neck and gently savoured the delicate pulse beating there.

Her bones melted, and she sank back against him, wanting more, much more.

'You're not playing fair.' The words emerged as a sibilant groan as he pressed her close in against him.

His arousal was a potent force, and the need to have him deep inside her was almost unbearable.

Michelle caught a glimpse of herself in the mirror, and almost gasped at the reflected image. She looked like a shameless wanton experiencing a witching ravishment.

Her eyes were large, the pupils dilated, and her lips had parted to emit a soundless sigh. Pink coloured her cheeks, and her body arched against his in silent invitation.

'Nikos, please.'

Without a word he grasped hold of her waist and lifted her to sit on the wide marbled vanity top, then he lowered his head to her breast and caressed one pale globe.

It was an erotic tasting that held her spellbound as she became consumed with treacherous sensation, and when she could bear it no longer she caught hold of his head and forced it up, then angled her mouth to his in a kiss that was urgent, hungry, and passionately intense.

How long before they slowly drew apart? Five minutes, ten? She had no idea. All she knew was that the slightest touch, the faintest sound, would tip them both past the point of no return.

It was Nikos who rested his forehead against her own as he effected a soothing circular movement over her shoulders.

'I guess we should take a raincheck, hmm?'

She wasn't capable of saying a word, and she looked faintly stricken as she inclined her head in silent acquiescence.

He cupped her face and kissed her gently, then he drew her down onto her feet. 'I'll go shower, shave and change.'

When he left she leaned both hands on the vanity and closed her eyes. She felt as if all her nerves had stretched to breaking point, and then shredded into a thousand pieces.

No man had ever had this effect on her before. Not once had she felt so *consumed,* so helpless. Or so deeply *involved.* It was frightening. For what happened when it ended, as it inevitably would? Could she walk away, and say, Thanks, it was great while it lasted?

The thought of a life without him in it seemed horribly empty.

You're bound to him, a tiny voice taunted. Until Saska relinquishes her widow's hold, and Jeremy has been removed, voluntarily or forcibly, from the picture.

So what do you suggest? she demanded silently. Love and live each day as if it's the last? That's the fiction. Reality will be a broken heart and empty dreams.

The sound of water running in the adjacent en suite acted as an incentive to gather herself together. She was a mess. Hair, make-up… She'd have to begin from scratch.

Michelle forced herself to work quickly, and after a shaky start she used expert touches to heighten her delicate bone structure, highlight her eyes, and outline her mouth.

Her hair was thick, and it wasn't difficult to add extra thickness with the skilful use of a brush and hair dryer.

The gown she'd chosen to wear was an ankle-length slinky black silk sheath with a softly draped bodice and slim shoestring shoulder straps. Black stiletto-heeled shoes completed the outfit, and she caught up a matching black stole, a small beaded evening bag, then walked out to the lounge.

Nikos was waiting for her, looking resplendent in a dark evening suit, white cotton pin-pleated shirt and black bow tie.

Michelle felt her heart stop, then quicken to a rapid beat. His broad facial bone structure lent him a primitive air, the chiselled cheekbones, dark eyes, the perfectly moulded nose, and a well-shaped mouth that could wreak such sensual havoc.

He was an impressive man, in a way that had little to do with the physical. There was a ruthlessness apparent that boded ill for anyone who dared to cross his path. There was also a gentleness that was totally in variance with his projected persona.

If he were to gift his heart to a woman, it would be a gift beyond price. A wise woman would treasure and treat it with care.

Such wayward thoughts were dangerous. She couldn't afford them, daren't even pause to give them a second of her time.

'Shall we leave?' She couldn't believe her voice sounded so steady, so cool.

The lift descended nonstop to the ground floor, the doors slid open to admit the receptionist before resuming its descent to the car park.

'Michelle. I put the flowers in a vase on the lobby side-table. It seemed such a pity to waste them. I hope you don't mind?' The lift slid to a halt and they emerged into the concrete cavern. 'Have a great evening.'

'What flowers?' Nikos queried as he led Michelle in the opposite direction towards his car.

'A bouquet of carnations.'

One eyebrow rose slightly. 'I'll rephrase that. Who sent you flowers?' He caught hold of her elbow and drew her to a halt when she didn't answer. 'Michelle?'

There didn't seem any advantage in prevaricating. 'Jeremy.'

Nikos' eyes hardened measurably. 'He delivered them personally?'

'Yes.'

'He spoke to you?' he demanded sharply.

'No. He merely stood outside and choreographed an elaborate bow.'

Nikos bit off a pithy oath. 'That young man seems to choose to dance with danger.'

She could almost feel the palpable anger emanate from his powerful frame as he unlocked the BMW, saw her seated, then he crossed round the car and slid in behind the wheel.

'Has he rung you at any time today?' He fired the engine, then eased the car towards the ramp.

'This evening, shortly after I arrived home.'

There was something primitive in his expression as he turned briefly towards her. 'Tomorrow morning we transfer to my apartment. And don't,' he warned bleakly. 'Argue. The penthouse can only be accessed by using a specially coded security key to operate the lift. Even the emergency stairwell is inaccessible from the floor below.' His eyes became hard and implacable. 'At least I know you'll be safe there.'

This was all getting a bit too much! 'Look—'

'It's not negotiable,' Nikos decreed with pitiless disregard.

'The hell it isn't!'

'We're almost there.'

He was right, she saw with amazement. It was less than two kilometres to the Marriott hotel, and they'd traversed the distance in record time.

'We'll discuss this later,' Michelle indicated as he cruised the car park for an empty
space.

'You can count on it,' Nikos agreed with
chilling bleakness.

Anger at his highhandedness tinged her
mood, and her back was stiff as she walked
at his side to the lift. There was a group of
fellow guests already waiting to be transported to the ballroom, and she forced her
facial muscles to relax as they rode the necessary two flights.

From that moment on it was strictly smile-
time as they mixed and mingled in the adjoining foyer. Uniformed waiters circulated
with trays loaded with champagne-filled
flutes, and she accepted one, sipped the sparkling liquid, and endeavoured to visually lo-
cate her parents.

'There you are.'

Michelle heard Saska's slightly accented
voice, summoned a smile, then she turned to
face the tall brunette.

'Saska,' she acknowledged politely. 'It's nice to see you.' How many mistruths did people utter beneath the guise of exchanging social pleasantries? Too many, she perceived cynically as she tilted her cheek to accept Emilio's kiss.

The guests began to dissipate as staff opened up the ballroom, and Michelle was supremely conscious of Nikos' arm along the back of her waist, the close proximity of his body as they moved slowly into the large room.

Circular tables seating ten were beautifully assembled with white linen, gleaming cutlery and glassware, beautiful floral centrepieces. Each table bore a number, and they gravitated as a foursome towards their designated seats.

Saska deliberately positioned herself next to Nikos, and Michelle was intensely irritated by the widow's deliberate action.

There was, unfortunately, very little she could do about it without causing a scene. A fact Saska had already calculated, and her smile was akin to that of a cat who'd just lapped a saucer of cream.

The evening's entertainment was to be broken into segments during the elaborate four-course meal, with a fashion parade as the conclusion.

Chantelle and Etienne Gerard joined them, together with two young couples. There was time for a brief round of introductions before the obligatory speech by the charity's fund-raising chairman, which was followed by a delicious French onion soup.

A magician dressed in elegant black, grey and white fatigues, white-painted face and black-painted lips demonstrated a brief repertoire with a multitude of different coloured scarves, silver rings, and a small bejewelled box.

A seafood starter was served, and Michelle nibbled at a succulent prawn, forked a few mouthfuls of dressed lettuce, then reached for the iced water.

Saska held Nikos' attention in what appeared to be a deep and meaningful conversation. Michelle caught Emilio's eye, saw his almost imperceptible wink, and felt her lips twitch.

He held no fewer illusions that she did. Emilio enjoyed the social scene, deriving cynical amusement from the many games of pretense the various guests played for the benefit of others. He was rarely mistaken in his assessment.

The starter dishes were collected by staff as the lights dimmed and a gifted soprano gave an exquisite solo performance from a popular opera.

Michelle sipped champagne and endeavoured to ignore the spread of Saska's beautifully lacquered nails on Nikos' thigh. The slight movement of those nails didn't escape her attention, and she felt the slow build of anger. And jealousy. Although she refused to acknowledge it as that emotion.

'Oh well done,' Saska accorded as the guests burst into applause.

Michelle watched her turn towards Nikos, say something in Greek, laugh, and touch the sleeve of his jacket.

Perhaps, she decided, it was time to play. The young man seated next to her was about her own age, and had partnered his sister to the function.

Michelle leaned towards him. 'I would say it's going to be a very successful evening.'

Two spots of colour hit his cheekbones. 'Yes. Yes, it is.' He indicated the soprano accepting a second round of applause. 'She's really quite something, isn't she?'

'Quite something,' Michelle agreed solemnly.

'The food is good, don't you think?' he rushed on earnestly. 'Can I help you to some wine? More champagne?'

She gave him a slow sweet smile. 'You could fill my water glass, if you don't mind.'

He didn't mind. In fact, he couldn't seem to believe his luck, given that the beautiful blonde who seemed to want to talk to him was in the company of a man whose power, looks and degree of sophistication were something he doubted he'd ever aspire to.

'Do you attend many of these charity functions?'

He was nice, pleasant and easy to talk to. 'My parents are very supportive of a few major charities,' she revealed. 'So yes, I attend a few each year.'

'Is—' he began awkwardly. 'Are you— Would you dance with me later?'

'I'd like that,' she said gently.

They were interrupted as the waitress deftly served the main course, and Michelle offered him a faint smile as she transferred her attention to the food.

She felt the light brush of fingers against her cheek, and she turned towards Nikos in silent query.

'He's just a boy,' he chided softly, and glimpsed the brilliant flare of gold in the depths of those beautiful green eyes.

'Are you saying,' she said with extreme care, 'that I shouldn't talk to him?'

'I doubt he's equipped to cope with your flirting.'

She met his gaze with composed tolerance. 'While you, of course, are well able to cope with Saska.'

'You noticed.' It was a statement, not a query, and she wanted to say she noticed everything about him. Except to acknowledge it would be tantamount to an admission of sorts, and she didn't want to betray her emotions.

He took hold of her hand and lifted it to his lips, then kissed each finger in turn. 'Eat, *pedhaki mou.*'

Dynamic masculinity at its most lethal, she accorded silently. All she had to do was look at him, and she became lost. It was if every cell in her body wanted to fuse with his, generating a sensual chemistry so vibrant and volatile, it was a wonder it didn't burst into flame.

'In that case, you'd better let me have my hand back,' she managed calmly, and glimpsed the musing gleam evident in those dark eyes so close to her own.

'Don't be too sassy,' Nikos drawled softly. 'Remember, we eventually get to go home together.'

'I'm trembling.'

'It will be my pleasure to ensure that you do.'

'Then I suggest you eat,' Michelle said demurely. 'You'll need the energy.'

One eyebrow slanted in visible amusement, and his eyes gleamed darkly.

'Darling,' she added, sotto voce, and pulled her hand free. She glanced up, caught Emilio's wicked expression, and widened her eyes in a deliberately facetious gesture.

Chicken and fish were served alternately, and she picked at the fish, speared the exotically presented vegetables, then pushed her plate forward. Dessert would follow, accompanied by a cheeseboard, and all she felt like was some fruit and cheese.

She picked up her glass and sipped the iced water, watching with detached fascination the precise movements as Nikos dealt with his food. He looked as if he took pleasure in the taste, the texture of each mouthful.

As he took pleasure in pleasing a woman. Just to see his mouth was to imagine it gliding slowly over her body, caressing soft skin, savouring each pulse beat. The sensual intimacy, the liberties he took, and her craven response.

Dear heaven, she could feel the blood course through her veins, heating her skin, just at the thought of what he could do to her.

Almost as if he sensed a subtle shift in the rhythm of her heart, he paused and slowly turned towards her.

For one millisecond, she was unable to mask the stark need, then it was gone, buried beneath the control of self-preservation, and his eyes darkened in recognition.

It felt as if there was no one else in the room, only them, and she could have sworn she swayed slightly, drawn towards him as if by some magnetic power.

Then he smiled. A soft widening of his mouth that held the hidden promise of what they would share.

She bit into the soft tissue of her lower lip, felt the slight stab of pain, and tasted blood. Her eyes flared, and the spell was broken. The room and its occupants reappeared, the sound of muted chatter, background music.

The waiters moved unobtrusively, removing dishes, plates, while a noted comedian took the microphone and wove jokes into stories with such flair and wit, it was impossible not to laugh.

Dessert comprised glazed strawberries in a chocolate basket decorated with fresh thickened cream. Sinful, Michelle accorded silently as she bit into the luscious fruit. She abandoned the chocolate and cream, and reached for the crackers and cheese as the compere announced the fashion parade.

Models took the stage in pairs, displaying an elegant selection of day wear, after five, and evening wear.

Coffee was served as the last pair of models disappeared from the stage, and it acted as a signal for the deejay to set up the music. It was also a moment when several guests chose to leave their respective tables to freshen up.

'Do you think—' a male voice inclined tentatively. 'Would you care to dance with me?'

Michelle turned towards him with a smile. 'Yes.' She placed her napkin on the table and rose to her feet.

He was good, very good, and she laughed as he led her into a set of steps she could only hope to follow. This was fun, *he* was fun, and for the next few minutes she went with the music.

'You do this very well,' she complimented as the music slowed to a more sedate beat.

'My sister and I are ballroom dancing competitors.'

'It shows,' she assured.

'I don't suppose—' He shook his head. 'No, of course not. Why would you?'

She looked at him and saw the enthusiasm of youth. 'Why would I *what?*' she queried gently.

'Agree to go out with me. The movies, a coffee. Anything.'

'If I wasn't with someone, I'd have loved to.'

'Really?' He could hardly believe it. 'You would?'

'Really,' she assured.

The track finished, and Michelle took the opportunity to thank him and indicate a return to their table.

CHAPTER ELEVEN

NIKOS met her eyes as she took the seat beside him, and he refilled her glass and handed it to her as the young man led his sister onto the floor.

'Did you let him down gently?'

'He asked me out.'

'Naturally you refused.'

She decided to tease him a little. Heaven knew he deserved it. 'I gave it considerable thought,' she said demurely. 'And I decided I would—' She paused deliberately, then offered an impish smile. 'Dance with him again.'

Nikos pressed a forefinger to the centre of her lips. 'Just so long as the last one is mine.'

'I'll try to remember,' she responded solemnly.

'Minx,' he accorded. 'Do you want some coffee?'

'I think so,' Michelle said solemnly. 'Any more champagne, and I might not be held responsible.'

His smile almost undid her. 'Responsible for what?'

'Doing Saska an unforgivable harm.'

'She's a friend.'

'I know, I know. It's just that the boundaries of her friendship with you seem to be expanding.'

'At the moment. Soon they'll shift back to their former position.'

'I admire your faith in human nature, but don't you think you're a little misguided?'

'No.'

A waitress appeared with a carafe of coffee and she poured them each a cup. Michelle reached for the sugar and stirred in two sachets.

'Nikos? Perhaps we could dance? Michelle, you don't mind, do you?'

She gave Saska a brilliant smile. 'Of course not. I intend to finish my coffee.'

'You and Nikos appear to be getting along together exceptionally well,' Chantelle inclined when Nikos and Saska had moved out of earshot.

She wanted to tell her mother the truth, but what was the truth? She wasn't sure any more. 'Yes,' she responded carefully. How would her mother react if she relayed they fought like hell on occasion and their lovemaking resembled heaven on earth?

Be amused, probably, offer a good argument cleared the air, and add the making up was always the best part.

'We're leaving soon, darling,' Chantelle relayed. 'It's quite late, and your father has an early flight to catch tomorrow. Maybe we could have lunch together? I'll call you, shall I?'

Nikos and Saska resumed their seats, and Michelle tried to ignore the arm he draped across the back of her chair. It brought him close and implied a deliberate intimacy.

'Please, *Maman*. I'll look forward to it.'

'Saturday, perhaps?'

'Not the weekend,' Nikos disputed. 'We'll be in Sydney.'

She cast him a challenging look. 'We will?'

'I have business there,' he enlightened with a mocking drawl that didn't fool her in the slightest.

'The break will do you good, *cherie,*' Chantelle enthused.

Since when had Nikos gained the God-given right to organise her life? Since he first walked into it, she acknowledged cynically.

Which didn't mean she'd simply give in without a struggle, and she said as much as he drew her on to the dance floor.

'I don't like being told what to do.'

'Especially by me, hmm?'

'Look—'

'No, *pedhi mou,*' Nikos stated with deceptive mildness. 'This is the way it is.' His eyes were at variance with his voice. 'Tomorrow I have a two o'clock meeting in Sydney, which will conclude with a social dinner. I plan to fly back to the Coast on Sunday. You get to go with me.'

'And just how do you propose to indicate my presence?'

His appraisal was swift, calculating, and brought a tinge of soft colour to her cheeks. 'I am answerable to no one.'

Michelle closed her eyes, then slowly opened them again. 'Well, now there's the thing. Neither am I.'

'Yes,' he refuted with silky tolerance. 'You are. To me. Until the situation with Jeremy is resolved.'

Anger and resentment surged to the surface, lending her eyes a brilliant sparkle. 'Let's not forget Saska in this scheme of things.'

An indolent smile curved the generous lines of his mouth. 'No,' he drawled with an edge of mockery. 'We can't dismiss Saska.'

Her back stiffened in silent anger. 'I don't think I want to dance with you.'

His lips brushed her temple, and his hands trailed a path up and down her lower spine in a soothing gesture.

'Yes, you do.'

Caught close in his arms wasn't conducive to conducting an argument, for she was far too conscious of the feel of that large body, the subtle nuances of sensation as her system went into overdrive.

'Always so sure of what I want, Nikos?'

His eyes held knowledge as he held her gaze. A knowledge that was infinitely sensual and alive with lambent passion. 'Yes.'

She was melting, subsiding into a thousand pieces, and there wasn't a sensible word she could frame in response.

His cologne combined with the scent of freshly laundered clothes and a barely detectable male muskiness. It proved a potent mix that attacked her senses, and she felt the need to be free of him, if only for the five or so minutes it would take to freshen up.

'I need to visit the powder room.'

It was late, and already the evening was beginning to wind down. In another hour the venue would close, and those inclined to do so would go on to a nightclub.

Michelle left the ballroom and entered the elegantly appointed powder room. After using the facilities, she crossed to the mirror to repair her make-up, and barely glanced up as the door swung in to admit another guest.

Saska. Coincidence, or design? Michelle opted for the latter.

'I have to hand it to you,' Saska complimented as she crossed to the mirror. 'You move quickly.'

No preamble, no niceties. Just straight to the heart of the matter.

'It's taken you less than a week to have Nikos delight in playing your knight in shining armour.'

Michelle capped her lipstick and placed it in her bag. 'I'm very grateful for his help.'

'Very convenient, these little episodes which have occurred with Jeremy.' She spared a glance at Michelle via the mirror, and one eyebrow arched in disbelief. 'You must agree it raises a few questions?'

'Are you accusing me of contriving a situation simply to manipulate Nikos' attention?'

'Darling, women are prepared to do anything to get Nikos' attention,' Saska declared with marked cynicism.

'Does that include you?'

'I would be lying if I said no,' Saska admitted.

Michelle drew in her breath and released it slowly. 'And the purpose of this little chat is?'

'Why, to let you know I'm in the race.'

'There is no race. Nikos isn't the prize.'

'You're neither naive nor stupid. So what game are you playing?'

'None,' Michelle said simply. 'Blame Nikos. He's the one intent on being the masterful hero, without any encouragement from me.' Without a further word she turned and left the room.

Nikos and Emilio were deep in conversation when she slid into her seat, and she met Nikos' swift glance with equanimity.

'More coffee?'

'Please.'

He signalled the waitress, and instructed her to refill both cups.

It was almost midnight when they left, and Michelle looked at the towering apartment buildings standing like sentinels against a dark sky. Lit windows provided a sprinkling of regimented light, and she wondered idly at the people residing there. A mix of residents and holiday-makers intent on enjoying the sun, surf and shopping available on this picturesque tourist strip.

Nikos paused at the lights, then turned into suburban Main Beach. Within minutes the car swept beneath her apartment building.

'I'm going to bed,' Michelle announced the instant Nikos closed the front door behind them.

'If you want to fight, then let's get it over and done with,' Nikos drawled with amusement.

She swung round to face him, and her chin tilted fractionally as she lifted one hand and began ticking off one finger after another. 'I'm not moving into your penthouse, and

I'm not—' she paused and gave the word re-petitive emphasis '—*not* spending the week-end in Sydney with you.'

'Yes, you are.'

She was on a roll, and unable to stop. 'Will you please do me a favour and inform Saska that I did not contrive to gain your attention by playing a *pretend assault* game with Jeremy!'

His eyes narrowed. 'She's—'

'Delusional,' Michelle accused fiercely.

'Temporarily obsessive,' Nikos amended.

'That, too!'

He crossed to where she stood and placed his hands on her shoulders, kneading them with a blissfully firm touch that eased the kinks.

Dear Lord, that felt good. Too good, she perceived. Any minute now she'd close her eyes, lean back, and give in to the magic of his touch.

His lips brushed against the sensitive hol-low at the edge of her neck, and she stifled a faint groan in pleasure.

She felt his fingers slide the shoestring straps over her shoulders, and the trail of kisses that followed them.

'This isn't going to resolve a thing,' Michelle inclined huskily as she acknowledged the slow curl of passion that began building deep inside. Any second now she wouldn't possess the will to resist him.

'Nikos, please—don't,' she almost begged as he kissed a particularly vulnerable spot at her nape.

'You want me to stop?'

No, but I daren't allow you to continue. Not if I want to retain any vestige of sanity.

'Yes,' she answered bravely. The loss of his touch made her feel cold, bereft, as she slowly turned to face him. Self-preservation caused her to move back a pace.

'I don't see the necessity for me to move into your penthouse. Removing myself to Sydney for the weekend is tantamount to running away. You're not responsible for me. What has happened with Jeremy would have happened anyway.' It came out sounding wrong, and Nikos used it to his advantage.

'You're saying you want to stay here alone,' he began with chilling softness. 'And risk having Jeremy utilise devious means and front up to your door? Or maybe lay in wait in the underground car park for the time you return home alone?'

His words evoked stark images from which she mentally withdrew. 'Suffer probable trauma as well as possible injuries? For what reason? Simply to prove you can protect yourself from an emotionally unbalanced young man with a history of previous attacks?'

Put like that, it sounded crazy. But what about *her* emotions? With each passing day she became more tightly bound to him on every level. What had begun as an amusing conspiracy was now way out of hand.

'You expect me to go to Sydney for the weekend, and spend every waking moment worrying if you're all right? Forget it.'

'Dammit. Why should it matter to you?'

His eyes hardened to a bleak grey. 'It matters.'

It was too much. *He* was too much. Without a word she crossed the lounge and entered her bedroom.

She closed the door, and wished fervently it held a lock and key. Although it would hardly prove an impenetrable barrier, for he possessed the brute strength to break the door down if he was so inclined.

With hands that shook she released the zip fastening at the back of her dress and slipped out of it. Next came her shoes, and she gathered up a cotton nightshirt and slipped it over her head.

It took only minutes to remove her make-up and brush her teeth, then she slid in between the sheets, snapped off the light to lay staring into the darkness.

Michelle had little knowledge of the passage of time as thoughts meshed with dreamlike images, and it was only when she stirred into wakefulness that she realised she must have fallen asleep.

She moved restlessly, and her hand encountered warm male flesh, hard bone and muscle. Her body went rigid with shock.

'Nikos?'

'Who else were you expecting, *melle mou?*' He brought her close and lowered his mouth to nuzzle the sweet hollows at the base of her throat, then trailed up to capture her mouth in a slow evocative kiss that stole her breath away.

It would be so easy to lose herself in his embrace, and she told herself she needed the warmth of his touch, the feel of him deep inside, and the mutual joy of lovemaking. At this precise moment she refused to label what they shared as *sex*.

Tomorrow she'd deal with when it dawned. But for now there was only the man and the wild sweet heat of his loving.

And the passion. Mesmeric, provocative, ravaging, until she went up in flames and took him with her.

*　　*　　*

Michelle rose early the next morning, then showered and dressed, she gathered together a selection of clothing suitable for a weekend in Sydney, added personal items and make-up, and packed them into a bag.

She'd considering making a final protest about the need to move into Nikos' penthouse, then dismissed it before she uttered a word. One look at his compelling features was sufficient to convince her that he intended to win any verbal battle she might choose to initiate.

'Leave your car here,' Nikos instructed as he stowed her bags in the boot of the BMW. The larger bag was destined to be deposited in the penthouse. 'I'll pick you up from the Gallery at ten.'

'OK.'

He shot her a musing glance. 'Such docility.'

'It's your forceful personality,' she assured sweetly. 'It has a cowering effect.'

His laughter was soft, husky, and sent renewed sensation spiralling through her body as she slid into the car beside him.

'No,' he mocked. 'It doesn't.' He fired the engine and sent the car up the ramp and onto the road.

It was at her insistence she spend an hour at the Gallery to dispense with some of the paperwork, rather than linger in her own or Nikos' apartment.

It was after midday when their flight touched down in Sydney, and almost one when they registered at an inner city Darling Harbour hotel.

'What do you plan to do this afternoon?' Nikos queried as he unfastened his garment bag and slotted it into the wardrobe.

'Shop,' Michelle declared succinctly as she followed his actions.

'I should be back by six. I'll make dinner reservations for seven.'

'Fine,' she acknowledged blithely, then gasped as he cradled her face and kissed her. Hard, and all too briefly.

He trailed gentle fingers along the lower edge of her jaw. 'I'll have my mobile if you need to contact me.' He caught up his suit jacket and pulled it on. 'Take care.'

Five minutes later Michelle took the lift down to reception, had the concierge summon a taxi, and she gave instructions to be driven to Double Bay.

The exclusive suburb was known for its numerous expensive boutiques housed in a delightful mix of modern glass-fronted shops and converted terrace cottages.

The sun shone, and the gentlest breeze stirred the leaves of magnificent old trees lining the streets.

Boutique coffee shops and trendy cafés with outdoor seating beneath sun umbrellas created a cosmopolitan influence.

Michelle pulled down her sunglasses from atop her head and prepared to do some serious shopping.

Two hours later she took a brief respite and ordered a cappuccino, then fortified, she caught up a selection of brightly emblazoned carry-bags and wandered through the Ritz-Carlton shopping arcade, paused to admire a display of imported shoes, fell in love with a pair of stilettos and after declaring them a perfect fit, she added them to her purchases.

It was after five-thirty when a taxi deposited her at the door of the hotel, and on entering their suite she took pleasure in examining the contents of numerous bags before storing them in the wardrobe.

With quick movements she gathered fresh underwear and a wrap, then escaped into the adjoining bathroom.

Nikos found her there, in a cloud of steam, her body slick with water, so completely caught up with her ablutions that she didn't even hear him enter.

The first Michelle knew of his presence was the buzz of his electric shaver, followed minutes later by the rap of his knuckles against the glass door as he slid the door open and stepped in beside her.

'Communal bathing, hmm?' she teased, loving the feel of his hands on her waist. 'Sorry to disappoint you, but I've nearly finished.'

'No, you haven't.' He slid his hands up over her ribcage and cupped each breast.

His fingers conducted an erotic teasing of each sensitive peak, and she felt desire arrow through her body.

'No?'

He didn't answer. He merely reached forward and closed the water dial, and she was incapable of saying another word as his mouth touched her own, teased, tasted, nibbled, then hardened with possessive masterfulness.

His tongue laved hers, and encouraged participation in an erotic dance that eventually became an imitation of the sexual act itself.

She wasn't conscious of leaning into him, or lifting her hands to hold fast his head. There was only the need to meet and match his passion until the heat began to dissipate.

Her skin was acutely sensitive to his slightest touch as he trailed gentle fingers back and forth across each collarbone, then slowly traversed to the slopes of her breasts.

His lips found the sweet hollow at the edge of her neck, and nuzzled. One hand splayed low over her abdomen, and caressed her hip, her buttock, then teased the soft curling hair at the apex between her thighs.

Michelle felt as if she was dying. A very slow erotic and incredibly evocative death as he brought her close to orgasm with tactile skill. Unbidden, her neck arched and a soft almost tortured moan escaped her throat as her feminine core radiated heat and ignited into sensual flame.

It was almost more than she could bear, and she cried out as he lifted her up against him. With one easy movement she linked her arms around his neck and wound her legs over his hips, glorying in the feel of him, the surging power, his strength.

Pagan, electrifying, primeval.

Michelle sensed the moment he let go, the slight shudder that shook his body, then the stillness, and she kissed him with such exquisite gentleness her eyes ached from unshed tears.

With infinite care they indulged in a long after-play, the light brush of fingers over sensitised skin, kisses as soft as the touch of a butterfly's wing.

She touched his face with the pads of her fingers, and slowly traced the strong bone structure with the care of someone who needed to commit his features to memory.

The firm eyebrows, broad forehead, the slightly prominent cheekbones and the wide firm jaw-line. She explored his lips, the clean curves, the firm flesh that could wreak such havoc at will.

Then she gave a soft yelp as he drew the tip of her finger into his mouth and gently nipped it.

Without a word he reached forward and turned on the water dial, set it at warm, then palmed the soap and began to smooth it over her body.

When he finished, she took it from his extended hand and returned the favour.

'Food,' Michelle inclined in a voice that shook slightly as he closed the water dial.

Nikos' eyes gleamed dark and his lips parted to form a musing smile. 'Hungry?' He leant forward and extracted a towel, draped it over her shoulders, then collected another and wound it round his hips.

'Ravenous.'

'Now wouldn't be a good time to tell you I've put our reservation back to eight.' He lifted a hand and smoothed a damp tendril of hair behind her ear. 'Or that we're joining three of my associates and their partners for dinner.'

She reached up and kissed his chin. 'I forgive you.'

'Do you, indeed?'

'Uh-huh.' Her eyes sparkled with devilish humour. 'I bought a new dress to wear tonight. And shoes.' She began to laugh. 'You get to see what I'm not wearing beneath it.' She wrinkled her nose at him. 'And suffer,' she added in an impish drawl.

'We can always leave early.'

He watched beneath hooded eyes as she went through the deodorant and powder routine, then she stepped into lacy thong bikini briefs, and his loins stirred into damnably new life.

She activated the hair dryer and brushed the damp curling length until it bounced thick and dry about her shoulders, then she began applying make-up.

If he stayed any longer, they wouldn't make it out of the suite, he perceived wryly. And for all that the evening was social, the prime criterion was business.

With that in mind he walked into the bedroom and began to dress.

When Michelle emerged from the bathroom all he had to do was fasten his tie and don his jacket.

She crossed to the wardrobe, extracted the dress, then stepped into it and turned her back to him.

'Would you mind?'

He moved forward and slid the long fastener closed over her bare skin. Minuscule briefs, no bra. Throughout the course of the evening he was going to go crazy every time he looked at her.

Michelle swung round to face him. 'What do you think?'

The cream silky sheath with an overlay of lace fell to just above her knees. Its scooped neckline was saved from indecency by a swathe of lace, and a single shoestring strap extended over each shoulder. Very high stiletto-heeled shoes in matching cream completed the outfit.

'You were right,' he drawled with an edge of mockery, and she laughed, a soft throaty sound that was deliciously sexy.

'It works both ways,' she assured with sparkling humour, and spared him an encompassing look.

Dark tailored trousers, blue shirt, navy silk tie, hand-stitched shoes. Expensive, exclusive labels that showed in the cloth and the cut. But it was more than that, she perceived a trifle wryly. The man wore them well, but it was the man himself who attracted attention. His height, breadth of shoulder, tapered waist, slim hips and long muscular legs would intrigue most women to wonder or discover if the physique matched up to the promised reality. Michelle could assure that it did.

He pulled on his suit jacket and extended a hand. 'Let's go.'

They took a taxi, got held up in traffic, arrived late, and opted to go straight to the table rather than linger at the bar.

In retrospect it proved to be a pleasant evening. Beneath the social niceties, it was clear that a deal had been struck and cemented during the afternoon. In Nikos' favour, Michelle perceived.

She found it intriguing to witness him in the executive role. He was a skilled tactician. His strategy was hard-edged, and she was reminded of the iron fist in a velvet glove analogy.

Tenacity, integrity. He possessed them both. His associates admired those qualities and lauded him for them. They also coveted his success.

It was after eleven when the bill was settled and they converged briefly outside the
entrance.

Nikos went to hail a taxi, only to pause
when Michelle caught hold of his hand.

'Our hotel is just across the causeway,' she
indicated, pointing it out. There were people
enjoying the warm summer evening. 'It's a
beautiful night. Why don't we walk?'

Nikos cast her a wry glance. 'In those
heels?'

'They're comfortable,' she assured. 'Besides, after that sumptuous meal we need the
exercise.'

'I think I prefer a ten-minute taxi ride to a
ten-minute walk.'

Her laughter was infectious. 'Conserving
energy, huh?'

'Something like that.' His drawl held musing mockery.

'And I thought you were at the peak of
physical fitness,' she teased unmercifully,
and laughed at his answering growl. 'We
walk?'

It took fifteen minutes because they paused midway to admire the city-scape. Myriad lights reflected in the dappled surface of the water, gunmetal in colour beneath the night sky. The air was fresh, tinged with the tang of the sea, and she felt the warmth of his arm as it curved along the back of her waist.

There was a part of her that wished this was real. That the sexual chemistry they shared was more, much more than libidinous passion.

How could you care deeply for someone in the space of a week? More than care, a tiny voice prompted. With each passing day she found it more difficult to separate the fantasy and the reality.

How much was pretense? Could a man kiss a woman so deeply, and not care? Make love with her so beautifully, and feel nothing more than sexual gratification?

And even if there is affection, is that all it would be?

Worse, when this is all over, what then?

What do you want? A convenient relationship for as long as it lasts? Then heartache? Don't kid yourself, she silently derided. Nikos doesn't want the *forever* kind, with a marriage certificate and children. Nor do you. Or at least, you didn't think you did until now.

Her life had been good until Nikos Alessandros walked into it. She'd been satisfied with the status quo. Content to run the Gallery jointly with Emilio. Happy in her own apartment, and with her social life.

Now, it didn't seem to mean as much.

Apprehension seeded and took root. How could she bear to live without him?

'Shall we continue?'

Michelle brought her attention back to the present and she tucked her hand into the crook of his elbow. 'Yes, let's go back.'

There was a sadness in the depths of her heart as they undressed each other and made love in the late hours of the night.

CHAPTER TWELVE

'DO YOU want to go down to breakfast, or shall we order in?'

'The restaurant,' Michelle said at once. 'Staying in could prove dangerous.'

'For whom, *melle mou?*'

'I might ravish you,' she teased mercilessly, and heard his soft mocking laughter.

'I tremble at the mere thought.'

'Well you might,' she threatened as she slipped from the bed, aware that he followed her actions.

'Today you have plans, hmm?'

Nikos sounded amused, and she picked up a pillow and threw it at him, then watched in fascination as he neatly fielded it. 'If you don't want to play, *pedhaki mou,*' he drawled, 'I suggest you go shower and dress.'

She escaped, only because he let her, and reemerged into the bedroom to quickly don elegantly tailored trousers and a deep emerald singlet top.

Nikos followed her actions, and after a superb breakfast they spent almost two hours in the Aquarium viewing the many varieties of fish displayed in numerous tanks before walking across the causeway to Darling Harbour to explore the many shops.

It was a beautiful summer's day, the sun shone, there was just the barest drift of cloud, and a gentle breeze to temper the heat.

They had lunch at a delightful restaurant overlooking the water, then they boarded a large superbly appointed catamaran for a cruise of Sydney harbour.

Mansions built on the many sloping cliff-faces commanded splendid city views, and the cruise director pointed out a few of the exceptionally notable residences nestling between trees and foliage.

Coves and inlets provided picturesque scenery, and there were craft of every size and description moored close to shore.

Sydney was famous for its Opera House, a brilliant architectural masterpiece instantly recognisable throughout the world, and its Harbour Bridge.

Of all the cities she'd visited, this one represented *home* in a vast continent with so many varying facets in its terrain. It tugged a special chord in the heart that had everything to do with the country of one's birth, patriotism and pride.

Nikos rarely moved from her side, and he appeared relaxed and at ease. The suit had been replaced by tailored trousers and a casual polo shirt which emphasised his breadth of shoulder, the strong muscle structure of his chest.

Michelle was supremely conscious of him, the light brush of his hand when they touched, the warmth of his smile.

Here, they were a thousand miles away from the Gold Coast, and Jeremy. Let's not forget Saska, she added wryly.

There was no need to maintain any pretense. So why hadn't Nikos abandoned the facade the moment they touched down in Sydney?

Because the sex is good? an inner voice taunted.

She should, she reflected, have insisted on separate suites. They could have each gone their separate ways for the entire weekend, then simply travelled to the airport together and caught the same flight to the Gold Coast.

So why didn't you? a silent voice demanded.

The answer was simple...she wanted to be with him.

Oh great, she mentally derided. Not only was she conducting a silent conversation, she was answering herself, as well.

It was almost five when the cruise boat returned to the pier, and afterwards they wandered at leisure along the broadwalk at Darling Harbour, and sat in one of many sidewalk cafés with a cool drink.

'Let's eat here,' Michelle suggested. The area projected a lively almost carnival ambience, and she loved the feel of a sea breeze on her face, the faint tang of salt in the air.

'You don't want to go back to the hotel, change, and dine *a deux* in some terribly sophisticated restaurant?' Nikos queried.

He looked relaxed, although only a fool would fail to detect the harnessed energy exigent beneath the surface.

'No,' she declared solemnly.

They ate seafood, sharing a huge platter containing a mixture of king-size prawns, mussels, oysters, lobster and Queensland crustaceans cooked in a variety of different ways, accompanied by several sauces and a large bowl of salad greens.

Dusk began to fall, and the city buildings took on a subtle change, providing a delightful night tapestry of light, shadow and increasing darkness.

'We could take in a movie, a show, visit the casino,' Nikos suggested as they emerged from the restaurant.

Michelle offered him a sparkling glance. 'You mean, I get to choose?'

'Last night was business,' he drawled, and she bit back a laugh.

'Not all of it.'

He took hold of her hand and linked his fingers between her own. 'Behave.'

'I shall,' she said demurely. 'Impeccably, for the next few hours. At the casino. Then,' she added with wicked humour, 'I plan to ravish you.'

'Two hours?'

'Uh-huh. It's called *anticipation*.'

It was worth the wait, Nikos accorded a long time later as he gathered her close on the edge of sleep. She'd made love with generosity and a sense of delight in his pleasure. And fun, before the intensity of passion had swept them both to a place that was theirs alone.

His arm tightened over her slender back, and she made a protesting murmur as she burrowed her cheek more deeply against his chest.

He soothed her with a gentle drift of his fingers, and brushed his lips against her hair, listening, feeling, as her breathing steadied into a deep even pattern.

'The Rocks,' Michelle chose without question when Nikos queried over breakfast what she would like to do with the day. Their flight to the Gold Coast was scheduled for midafternoon.

'Trendy cafés, shops, and—'

'Ambience,' she intercepted with a wicked smile.

They took a taxi, and spent a few pleasant hours wandering the promenade, examining the various market stalls, chose a café where they enjoyed a leisurely meal, then it was time to return to the hotel, collect their bags and head for the airport.

With each passing hour she felt an increasing degree of tension. And sadness the weekend was fast approaching a close.

'Thank you,' she said quietly as they waited for their bags to arrive on the carousel from the flight. 'It was a lovely break away.'

Nikos glimpsed the subtle edge of apprehension apparent, and divined its cause. A muscle hardened along the edge of his jaw. Jeremy's behaviour pattern was predictably unpredictable. His parents' method of dealing with their son's recurring problem, however, was not.

For the past week he'd deliberately scaled down his business commitments to an essential few, and chosen to work via the computer link-up in his apartment, instead of his company office overlooking the Southport Broadwater.

Nikos sighted their bags and lifted them off the carousel. Five minutes later he was easing the large BMW out from the security car park.

'Do you mind if I make a phone call?' Michelle queried soon after they entered the penthouse.

'Go ahead. I'll be in the study for an hour.'

She rang her mother, put a call through to Emilio, then she retreated to the bedroom to unpack.

*   *   *

Michelle left early the next morning for the Gallery, and by midday she'd managed to catch up with most of the paperwork. Lunch was a sandwich washed down with mineral water and eaten at her desk.

Preliminary festive season parties were already under way, and tonight they were to join her parents and several of her father's associates for dinner at the Sheraton.

It was after five when she entered Nikos' penthouse, and after a quick shower she tended to her make-up, swept her hair into a smooth French pleat, then she donned a cobalt blue fitted dress with a sheer printed overlay, slid her feet into stiletto-heeled shoes, and collected her evening purse.

'OK, let's go.'

'There's something you should know before we leave.'

Her smile faltered slightly. 'Bad news?'

'Jeremy and his parents left the country early this morning. Their home is up for sale, and Emerson's office is closed.'

'Thank God,' she breathed shakily, as surprise mingled with relief.

'Rumour has it they intend settling in Majorca.'

It was over! She could hardly believe it. No longer would she have to look over her shoulder, suspect every shadow, or be apprehensive each time the phone rang. She could resume a relatively carefree life, move back into her apartment...

Nikos caught each fleeting expression and successfully divined every one of them.

A weight sank low in her stomach as comprehension dawned. Nikos' protection was no longer necessary. Which meant—*what?* Did she thank him, then walk out of his life? *Would he let her?*

'The news has already leaked and speculation is rife,' Nikos said quietly. 'I wanted you to hear it from me, rather than an exaggerated version from someone else.'

'Thank you.'

He could sense her tentative withdrawal, see the hidden uncertainty, and he wanted to shake her.

'We'd better leave,' Michelle said brightly. '*Maman* said six-thirty.' It was almost that now.

It was a beautiful evening. Except she didn't really *see* the azure blue of the sky as Nikos drove the short distance to the Sheraton hotel.

Michelle drew in a deep breath, then slowly released it as he slid from the car and consigned it to the concierge's care for valet parking.

She'd have to go inside and act her socks off in an attempt to portray an air of conviviality.

It didn't help to discover Saska was present in the company of one of her father's business associates. Although it was hardly surprising given the associate had been a guest on the same night as Saska at her parents' home the previous week.

Champagne on an empty stomach was not a wise move, and her appetite diminished despite the superb seafood buffet. While everyone else filled their plates and returned for more, all she could manage to eat was a few mouthfuls of salad and two prawns.

Michelle conversed with apparent attentiveness to the subject, but within minutes she retained only a hazy recollection of what had been said.

Her mind was consumed with Nikos as she reflected on every detail, each sequence of events that had brought and kept them together.

She reached out and absently fingered the stem of her champagne flute.

'Michelle?'

Oh Lord, she really would have to concentrate! She looked across the table and saw Saska's bemused expression. 'I'm sorry,' she apologised. 'What did you say?'

'I'm leaving for Sydney tomorrow to spend a few weeks with friends before flying home to Athens.'

Sydney, *Athens?* Saska was leaving the Gold Coast *tomorrow?* Her brain whirled. Did that mean Saska had given up any hope of turning Nikos' affection into something stronger, more permanent?

'I'm sure you'll enjoy Sydney,' she managed politely. 'There are so many things to see and do there.'

'I'm looking forward to it.'

Michelle wasn't sure how she managed to get through the rest of the evening. She even managed to pretend to eat, and followed mineral water with two cups of very strong coffee.

It was after eleven when Etienne settled the bill and brought the evening to a close. Some of the guests had taken advantage of valet parking, others had chosen to park in the underground car park. Consequently farewells and festive wishes were exchanged in the main lobby.

Within minutes of emerging from the main entrance the concierge had organised Nikos' car, and Michelle sat in silence during the short drive.

The penthouse had been a haven, now it seemed as if she was viewing it for the last time. Dammit, she daren't submit to the ache of silent tears.

She was breaking up, fragmenting into countless pieces. Tomorrow... Dear heaven, she didn't want to think about tomorrow.

Nikos lifted a hand and tilted her chin, then held fast her nape as he angled his mouth over hers in a kiss that tore at the very depths of her soul.

It became a bewitching seduction of all her senses, magical, mesmeric, and infinitely flagrant as he led her deeper and deeper into a well of passion.

There was something almost wild about their lovemaking, a pagan coupling filled with raw desire and primitive heat.

Afterwards Michelle lay quietly in Nikos' arms, listening to his heart as it beat in unison with her own.

Then when she was sure he slept, she carefully eased herself free and slid from the bed.

She moved quietly into the kitchen, found a glass, filled it with water, then drank it down in the hope it would lessen the caffeine content of the coffee.

For the life of her she couldn't return to that large bed and pretend to sleep. Without thought she crossed to the lounge and moved the drape a little so she could see the night sky and the ocean.

CHAPTER THIRTEEN

'PENNY for them?'

Michelle turned her head at the sound of that drawling voice, and her stomach did a backward flip as he linked his arms around her waist and pulled her back against him.

'It's all worked out well,' she managed evenly. 'The Bateson-Burrows have relocated, and—'

'Saska has reevaluated her options, and accepted I'm not one of them,' Nikos drawled as he rested his chin on top of her head.

So where does that leave us?

Fool, she accorded silently. Where do you think it leaves you? You'll go back to your own apartment. Nikos will remain in his— until he returns to Athens, or settles in France, or any other European city where he has a base.

Sure, he might promise to call, and maybe he will, once or twice. He'll simply take up with any one of several beautiful females, and continue with his life. While you fall into a thousand pieces.

The mere thought of him with another woman made her feel physically ill.

'I should thank you,' Michelle said quietly. 'For everything you've done to help protect me from Jeremy.'

The night sky held a sprinkle of stars, pin-pricks of light against dark velvet, and less than a kilometre distant the marina stood highlighted beneath a series of neon arcs.

If I tried really hard, she thought dully, I could count some of the stars. Perhaps I should wish on one of them. Although wishes rarely came true, and belonged to the fable of fairy tales.

'I consider myself thanked.'

Did she detect a slight edge of mockery in his voice? Dear God, of course she had thanked him. With her body, from the depths of her soul, every time they'd made love.

She was almost willing to swear that their lovemaking had meant something more to him than just a frequent series of wonderfully orgasmic sexual experiences.

Women faked it. But were men capable of faking that ultimate shuddering release?

Nikos possessed control…but he'd lost it on more than one occasion in her arms, just as she'd threshed helplessly in his against an erotic tide so tumultuous she was swept way out of her depth. Only to be brought back to the safety of his embrace.

'I'll pack and move into my apartment in the morning.'

Was that her voice? It sounded so low, so impossibly husky, it could have belonged to someone else.

'No.'

Michelle's heart stopped, then accelerated to a rapid beat. 'What do you mean—*no*?'

His hands moved up to her shoulders. 'Do you want to leave?'

Dear heaven, how could he ask such a question?

She was incapable of movement, and he slowly turned her to face him.

'Michelle?'

'I—how—' Oh hell, she was incapable of putting two coherent words together. 'What are you suggesting?' she managed at last.

'I want you to come with me when I fly out to New York.'

Want, not *need*, she noted dully.

Did she have any idea how transparent she was? Eyes so clear he glimpsed his reflected image in their depths. A pulse hammered at her temple, and was joined by another at the base of her throat.

Go, an inner voice urged. Enjoy the *now,* and don't worry what will happen next month, next year. Just…hop on the merry-go-round and enjoy the ride for as long as it lasts.

But what happens when the music winds down and the merry-go-round slows to a stop? Would the break be any easier then, than it is now? Worse, she knew. Much, much worse.

Yet life itself came with no guarantees. If she walked away now, she'd never know what the future might hold.

It was no contest. There could be only one answer.

'Yes,' Michelle said simply.

Nikos covered her mouth with his own in a kiss so incredibly gentle, she wanted to cry.

'There's one more thing.'

He pressed his thumb over her lower lip. 'Marry me, *agape mou.*'

Her eyes widened measurably, and for an instant her whole body stilled, then she became conscious of the loud hammering of her heart and the need to breathe.

'Yes.'

His smile almost undid her. 'No qualifications?'

Michelle shook her head, not trusting herself to speak.

'How do you feel about a Celebrant marrying us in the gardens of your parents' home two weeks from this Saturday?'

She did swift mental calculations. 'Two days before Christmas?' Dear heaven. 'My mother will freak.'

He stroked the rapidly beating pulse at the base of her throat. 'No, she won't.'

Two weeks. 'Nikos—'

'I love you,' he said gently. 'Everything about you. The way you smile, your laughter, the sound of your voice. The contented sigh you breathe when you reach for me in the night.' His mouth settled briefly on hers. 'I need you to share my life, all the days, the nights. Forever.'

Michelle closed her eyes in an attempt to still the sudden rush of tears. 'I knew you were trouble the first moment I set eyes on you,' she stated shakily.

'An arrogant Greek who took control and turned your life upside down, hmm?'

Stifled laughter choked in her throat. 'Something like that.' Her eyes gleamed with remembered amusement. 'You were always there, in my face.' Her expression sobered momentarily. 'Thank God.'

'Fate, *pedhaki mou.*' He cupped her face and smoothed away the soft trickle of tears with each thumb. 'It put us both in the same place at the same time.'

Yes, but it had been more than that, she acknowledged silently.

Much more.

'You never did intend this arrangement to be temporary, did you?'

He dropped a soft kiss onto the tip of her nose.

'No.'

'When did you decide?'

'I walked into the Bateson-Burrows' home that first evening, took one look at you, and knew I wanted to be in your life.'

'Why?'

He smiled, a self-deprecatory gesture that was endearing in a man of his calibre. 'Instinct. Then Fate dealt me a wild card.'

'Which you didn't hesitate to use,' she acknowledged musingly.

'Do you blame me?'

Michelle lifted her arms and linked her hands at his nape, then she drew his head down to hers. 'I love you,' she said with quiet sincerely. 'I always will. For as long as I live.'

'Come back to bed.'

She couldn't resist teasing him a little. 'To sleep?'

'Eventually.' He kissed her with hungry possession. 'After which we'll rise and face the first of several hectic days.'

Nikos had been right, Michelle mused as she kissed her mother, then hugged Etienne.

Each day had proven to be more hectic than the last. Yet superb organisation had achieved the impossible by bringing everything together to make their wedding day perfect.

There had been tears and laughter as the Celebrant pronounced them man and wife, and Nikos kissed the bride.

Photographs, the cutting of the cake, and an informal reception had completed the afternoon.

Now it was time to leave in the elegant stretch Cadillac hired to transport them to a Brisbane hotel where they'd stay prior to catching an international flight early the next morning.

'We made it,' Michelle said jubilantly as the driver eased the long vehicle away from Sovereign Islands towards the arterial road leading to the Pacific Highway. From there, it was a forty-five-minute drive to Brisbane city.

Nikos took hold of her hand and raised it to his lips. 'Did you think we wouldn't, *agape mou?*'

Her smile melted his heart. 'Not for a moment. You and my mother make a formidable team.'

He kissed the finger which held his rings, and praised his God for the good fortune in finding this woman, his wife.

When he reflected on the circumstance, the chance meeting, and how close he had come to delegating his trip to Australia... It made his blood run cold to think he might never have met her, never experienced the joy of her love or had the opportunity to share her life.

He had never seen her look as beautiful as she did today. The dress, the veil, they merely enhanced the true beauty of heart and soul that shone from within.

A man could drown in the depths of those brilliant deep green eyes, and be forgiven for thinking he'd died and gone to heaven when those soft lips met his own.

'Champagne?'

Michelle looked at the man seated close beside her, and gloried in the look of him. There was inherent strength apparent, an indomitability possessed by few men. She wanted to reach out and trace the groove that slashed each cheek, trail the outline of his firm mouth, then have those muscular arms hold her close.

'No.' She leaned against him and laid her head into the curve of his shoulder.

'Tired?'

'A little.'

'We'll order in room service, and catch an early night.'

She smiled at the delightful vision that encouraged. 'Sounds good to me.'

Nikos lifted a hand and threaded his fingers through the length of her hair, creating a soothing massage that had a soporific effect.

'Did I tell you we're spending two weeks in Paris after I've concluded meetings in New York?'

'Paris?' The Arc de Triomphe, the Eiffel Tower, the ambience that was the soul of France.

'Paris,' he reiterated. 'A delayed honeymoon.'

'Now I know why I fell in love with you.'

'My undoubted charm?' he mocked lightly, and felt her fingers curl within his.

'The essence that is Nikos Alessandros, regardless of wealth and possessions. *You,*' she emphasised.

'There is an analogy that states "'tis woman who maketh the man."'

'I think it's reciprocal,' she accorded with wicked amusement.

Michelle lapsed into reflective silence.

Everything had been neatly taken care of. She'd arranged to lease out her apartment; together, she and Emilio had interviewed several people to act as her replacement at the Gallery, and had finally settled on a competent knowledgeable young woman who would, unless Michelle was mistaken, give Emilio a run for his money.

She intended to liaise with Emilio from wherever she happened to be in the world. New York, Paris, Athens, Rome. In this modern technological age, distance was no longer an important factor.

It was almost dark when the Cadillac slid to a halt outside the main entrance to their hotel. Check-in took only minutes, then they rode the lift to their designated suite.

Flowers, champagne on ice, fresh fruit and an assortment of Belgian chocolates were displayed for their enjoyment, and Michelle performed a sedate pirouette and went straight into Nikos' waiting arms.

His kiss was both gentle and possessive, a gift and a statement which she returned twofold.

'Mmm,' she teased. 'I could get used to this.'

'The hotel suite?'

'You—me. Sharing and working at making a life together. Happiness, *love.*'

'Always,' Nikos vowed. His mouth fastened over hers, and he deepened the kiss, exulting in her response until their clothes were an unbearable restriction.

'I guess we don't get to eat for a while,' Michelle murmured as she nibbled his ear.

'Hungry?'

'Only for you.' Always, only you, she silently reiterated.

Love. The most precious gift of all, and it was theirs for a lifetime.

MILLS & BOON® PUBLISH EIGHT
LARGE PRINT TITLES A MONTH.
THESE ARE THE EIGHT TITLES
FOR MARCH 2000

———————— ❧ ————————

MARRIAGE ULTIMATUM
Lindsay Armstrong

MISTRESS BY ARRANGEMENT
Helen Bianchin

BARTALDI'S BRIDE
Sara Craven

TO TAME A BRIDE
Susan Fox

THE SICILIAN'S MISTRESS
Lynne Graham

BRIDEGROOM ON APPROVAL
Day Leclaire

SLADE BARON'S BRIDE
Sandra Marton

HUSBAND POTENTIAL
Rebecca Winters

MILLS & BOON®

Makes any time special™